* * * *

'IT'S... SHARKS!'

by Rob Brenton

Warcry Publishing... *"There are beautiful things in life if you are prepared to see, listen and learn... There's more to life than mucky books and 'The Beano'."*

'26,107 words of infuriating graft.'

- Rob Brenton, June 2018

* * * *

'IT'S... SHARKS!'

PAUL SYKES
&
THE STRAITS OF JOHOR

A Short Story
by Rob Brenton ©

facebook.com/warcrypublishing

"Not Shark infested, but none of the locals go paddlin"

- Paul Sykes, circa 1990

'IT'S... SHARKS!' PAUL SYKES & THE STRAITS OF JOHOR

ISBN: 978-1-912543-13-7

All rights reserved. No part of this publication may be reproduced or transmitted in any form or by any means, including photocopying and recording, without the written permission of the copyright holder, application for which should be addressed to the publisher via the dealing agent at warcypress@roobix.co.uk. Such written permission must also be obtained before any part of this publication is stored in a retrieval system of any nature. This book is sold subject to the Standard Terms and Conditions of Sale of New Books and may not be re-sold in the UK below the net price fixed by the Publisher / Agent

Produced by Warcry Press (part of Roobix Ltd) on behalf of Rob Brenton, Knottingley (c) 2018.

Printed and bound in Great Britain by the PMM Group, Leeds

Book Cover Design by Gavin Parker Art – gavinparker.uk

Dennis Flint / Paul & Shark images by James Foreman - cargocollective.com/jamesryanforeman

Find out more at: facebook.com/warcrypublishing

NOTE:

'It's... Sharks!' Paul Sykes & The Straits of Johor is a work of fiction. Names, characters, businesses, events and incidents are the products of the author's imagination. Any resemblance to actual persons, living or dead, or actual events is purely coincidental... Yeah, Reyt!?

truculent; *eager or quick to argue or fight; aggressively defiant.*

INTRODUCTION (1985)

Left alone in the silence of that filthy little room, I was beginning to wonder if I'd ever get out. It was worse than any punishment cell I'd ever been in and a million miles away from the five star retreat I'd been staying at only a few days previous.

Not a single window and the heat from the sun had been turned all the way up to full. I wanted to lie on the floor and die, when without warning the door opened and all thoughts of death imploded, my senses instantly alert and stood back to attention once again.

"Time to go Mistah Sykes." The squinty-eyed authoritarian squealed in his imitation English. The look on his face telling me he was unsure himself if what he had just said made any sense at all.

I walked the narrow corridor with trepidation. The walls clearly painted to government approval, I bet there were a thousand more looked exactly the same. It was silent and sad, as if the short concrete floor with doors either side were a morgue for dead dreams. Everywhere you looked there were statutory rights being obliterated.

I waited impatiently for another screw to unlock the next security door. What a fucking dump I thought. A more depressing, miserable nick couldn't be found than this.

"See you in three days Mistah Sykes." He grinned, a grin so evil he could have had horns growing from the top of his head.

With that he swivelled on his heel and disappeared in a cloud of smoke, returning the way he'd come without so much as a backward glance and mumbling something in

Mandarin. Something I'd loosely translated to mean an animal like me shouldn't really be in prison, I should have my arms off at the elbow, my legs off at the knees and be released back into the wild to fail miserably. He was entitled to his opinion and invariably many would say the same.

BANG! The Judas gate slammed behind me. A sound enough to catapult me through the busy market streets of Bugis and across the Straits of Johor to freedom.

The little nip had slid back into the safety of the nick and peered through the door's viewing port, leering arrogantly like a screw who'd just pressed the panic button after a con had refused to sew mail-bags. Go on ye daft cunt, I thought, lock yourself in. Their (screws) stupidity amazed me at times. I'd fucking kill him. I'd rip his fucking head off and smash his ribs in if I ever came back, hopefully that wouldn't happen, for both our sakes.

He looked a real peasant from the Shangtung jungle, an ugly little sod, clearly born with far too many teeth in his head. I knew what vindictive bastards these lot could be, the language or continent wasn't relevant.

I had two pathetic days to sort this shitty mess out. I knew what I had to do, put some distance between myself and that place as soon as I could. The alternative? Spending the rest of my life holed up in that rat infested sanctuary to the damned they called Changi nick.

My exit and new-found freedom, albeit temporary, gave me a feeling so powerful I could shift the great pyramids on a wheelbarrow, and if I could cross those waters over to the mainland then I might just make that my next challenge.

I scoured my surroundings. It was time to get a move on. I needed a sign, not one delivered by god, none of that Christian pretending shit, something more practical and I found it in the form of a battered old road sign, pointing the way to Sembawang Park...

CHAPTER ONE

'THE PENGUIN COLONY'

Prior to my arrest I'd been staying at the Goodwood Park Hotel on Scotts Road for the best part of two weeks.

A distinguished five star heritage hotel offering unparalleled hospitality, luxurious accommodation and renowned cuisine, you get the picture.

It was the first decent hotel I'd clapped eyes on upon leaving the subway station and would clearly be way outside the realms of my budget within a matter of hours, especially the way I lived.

When I'd arrived the Goodwood was positively heaving. A penguin-colony of fellers in evening dress, white pullovers and top jolly evening suits.

As I navigated my way to the bar I didn't encounter one familiar English face. Every nation from around the world was being represented here, but none stood out so much as a 6' 3" Neanderthal from the backwaters of Wakefield.

Those penguin clad snides thought we all still lived in caves. I'd show them all about cave-men from Wakefield, the best little city on earth.

I checked in without too many problems, made my way up to my room on the 5th floor and slung my bag on the carpet to claim the space, just like a nick changing room.

I immediately felt at home, my own little space. I didn't have to share with someone who snored, whose feet stank, who asked too many questions, it was bliss.

I slept the entire first night on the balcony, staring up at the stars and wondering if I'd truly found my Shangri-la. I'd felt the same sense of completion I had the nights I'd spent star gazing up on the Helipad at Pinderfields General. It had always helped me to forget about my problems and avoid the anarchy of my life, until it was needed, then all hell would break loose, but not here, not now.

I'd paid for the room initially using £600 I'd borrowed from some friends (snigger) before leaving the UK. But since I'd arrived I'd been hitting the local bars hard; The Obar Punggol, The Yard, Zouk, Molly Malone's I'd even been over to the palatial Raffles for the afternoon, but that hadn't ended well. I'd been asked to leave and on that rare occasion I'd chosen to listen.

I'd got a taste for it, the wonderful weather, beautiful surroundings and my new-found audience in the locals spurred me on.

As my cash supply started to dwindle I had no option but to make an example of the Hotel's flippant credit arrangements. I hadn't set out to, but my all consuming nature and immoral ways meant it was only a matter of time before the place went into liquidation.

I'd been in a state of almost permanent intoxication, sloshed for want of a better term, since my arrival, hardly noticing the attention I was attracting in the hotel. It was peculiar how booze affected me. I didn't wobble, slur my speech, cry, laugh, or do any of the things people usually do under the influence, and to say I'd never really boozed in my life up until this point, I had a remarkable ability to consume it by the bucketful. It numbed my senses and brought a blissful state of relief and eventually a whole world of problems to boot.

I'd ruptured a kidney in 1968 playing football and I needed about twelve pints of fluid everyday just to keep it in a state of hydration, I wasn't one to suffer the embarrassment of asking for a tap water.

I had no real intention of clearing the bill at 'The Goodwood'. I'd become accustomed to avoiding restaurant and bar bills back home in a way that was positively award winning and it didn't worry me in the slightest out here, though deep down I knew it couldn't be sustained. The timing of my exit would be critical to not having to pick up the pieces further down the line.

What I thought would be my 'new life' in the sun, was quickly beginning to turn sour. Within a few days the loneliness of my surroundings, beautiful as they were, had turned everyone and everything against me. Six thousand miles from home, nobody, no family, nothing. All I wanted to do was get drunk and escape my demons, the same ones that had chased me through the streets of Wakefield. The coppers, the screws, the women, the promoters, the same demons I thought hadn't made it on to the plane with me to Singapore.

I drifted for another week or so in an alcoholic haze, one day to the next, in an attempt to push those demons into the backwash at the base of my brain.

I was sailing far too close to the wind, not caring about anyone or anything, just like I had many times before back in the UK, and that could never last.

Wallowing in self-pity like a big tart and getting myself into a lot of trouble in the process. I'd be as infamous in Singapore as I was on the Lupset Estate before the week was out.

It wasn't long before my ferocious appetite for the Barsac and lairy ways were being noticed by the staff at the Hotel and questions were being asked. How was this giant ape going to cover his bill? A valid question indeed and one with an answer I had yet to figure out myself.

They'd initially thought I was a governor or a CEO, because of the pin-stripes, but I was 'brassic' beneath, all fur-coat and no knickers, and it was starting to show. My mask slowly being stripped to reveal the penniless vagrant underneath. Something was now clearly amiss.

I'd been tipping the concierge heavily, to keep the heat from myself. That had kept the 'real' bills at bay for nearly a week, 'Gotta look after the little man.' I fannied myself.

But eventually they'd sussed me out. My whole stay at that hotel was a farce akin to a Blackpool side-show.

The Manager and a couple of his more menacing looking kitchen staff eventually took umbrage and decided to confront me, coincidentally with their tools of trade still about their person.

They had caught me off guard, just about to leave. Erupting with threats and derision the likes of which I had never encountered before. They took things personally out here, was it really their hotel? I doubted it, but it appeared that way.

The head chef pulled out a carving knife big enough to sever an Elephant's leg and said 'Just in case you start,' or something to that effect and duly waved it under my nose.

Given five minutes alone with him I'd make him wish he'd 'foot' the bill himself, at S$16,000 (Singapore Dollars) he was likely to struggle, a handsome sum by anyone's standards. I hadn't recalled buying the entire hotel a drink, or indeed urinating in the reception area's ornamental plant pots, but the evidence was there on the printed bill and the dot matrix rarely lied.

The extreme taxation of alcohol in Singapore made it nearly impossible to get woozy without going broke. I'd refused to pay purely out of lack of options, though my principles (or lack of) would have never allowed that anyway.

"Maybe I could work the kitchens and pay it off." I sniggered.

I was sure the police were already on their way and resistance would now be somewhat futile. I played the petrified business man in an Oscar winning performance Oliver Reed would be hard pushed to better.

The manager, an officious little prick, for want of a better term, with a face like a bad ham and an attitude to match, wasn't such a bad actor himself. As I recalled he'd been a lot more amenable whilst on the receiving end of the complimentary Gin Sling's I'd shouted him only the night before. How quickly these little nips forgot.

It was a man's right to get drunk, but he was not allowed to get disorderly but I'd abused the privilege to the tune of a S$16,000 headache that wasn't going away any time soon.

My mind started going in to overdrive. The penalty for an act like this had to be a jail term of up to six months plus a minimum of three strokes of the cane. Back home I could handle that, but out here I wasn't quite sure.

Before I knew it I was slung in the back of the Singha meat wagon and on my way to the local station to explain myself. Where would I begin?

CHAPTER TWO

'IT WAS EITHER THAT OR CHANGI NICK'

Those fucking lousy slants had me locked up for four days over that poxy bar bill.

I'd been arrested, charged, and remanded in custody, or the Singha equivalent, and now had only a precious few days to rectify the situation, it was either that or Changi nick.

Changi gaol houses some of Singapore's most serious criminals, including those serving long stretches and some sentenced to death, usually by hanging and traditionally on a Friday morning. Today was Saturday and that was a relief, I'd hate to have been drafted in just to meet the weekly quota.

They'd questioned me relentlessly for the past few days; Where I'd been, Why was I there, How was I gonna go about making matters right? Desperately trying to get to the bottom of my intentions in their beloved country. Truth was, I had no real intentions, apart from not to return to the nick back home.

I'd elected not to invoke my right to assistance from the British Embassy, for obvious reasons and much to their puzzlement. They knew something wasn't right but couldn't quite put their finger on it, but it was easier not to try and hence the reason I'd been given three days pardon to rectify the situation.

I'd explained my problems away under the guise that it wouldn't be good for my reputation back home to be caught up in such events. A wonderful citizen like me would be crucified publicly by the Wakefield Express if word got out, momentarily making the Express sound more elaborate than The Sun or The Daily Mirror.

During the interrogation my brain retained its general good form, computing quicker than lightning as I reeled off the fable of a well to-do business man relieved of his essentials in a land far, far away from home.

A woeful tale of cancelled credit cards and sleepless nights that could melt even a copper's black-heart. The assurity that my wealthy friends back in the UK would help sort the situation out adding to the yarn.

It would 'simply' take me a day or two to make arrangements for the funds to be transferred over. The hotel would be recompensed, and some, and I would be on my merry way. To add effect I didn't stop for one minute telling them how pathetic I was, and it appeared to be doing the trick.

They were clearly buying it for now. I'd been wearing my usual attire of a three-piece pin-stripe suit when they'd pulled me, trying to portray the image of a rugger-playing barrister. I had a couple of different suits for different occasions but all of them were three-piece and pin-striped. I worked in one, I played in one. I liked suits and so did my Cath.

I'd done my best to retain my composure under interview, mildly losing my temper only a couple of times with the pompous officials stood in my path.

"I'm not playing, some kind of game it is, I don't know what kind of game, but I'm not playing" I'd barked, before quickly regaining my sanity and reigning myself back in for my own good.

Even a blind man could see I wasn't telling the truth, but they had to give me the benefit of the doubt, plus it would be far less paperwork and aggravation if I could rectify the situation for them.

The language barrier was beginning to frustrate all concerned, and my stereotypical Chinese takeaway owner impersonations were failing miserably to convert to anything meaningful or indeed help matters at all.

I'd been given bail of sorts, my pleas reinforced by the fact that I was a close friend of the ex-mayor of Castleford Mr. Burt Corris, who would stand surety for me and vouch of my good character. What did they know? These idiots were under the impression he was next in line to the throne.

I'd been lucky, I knew the powers of the police were unlimited and they could do exactly what they wanted. I'd had a stroke of luck out here, another clean break was ready to ruin.

*   *   *   *

I'd already burnt my bridges whilst on license back home in the UK and skipped off to Singapore. I say skipped it was a bit more of a stumble and a trip, what a bloody debacle. You'd think they'd want rid of me, not make it fuckin difficult. That's the British police force' mentality for you; waste another few grand of the tax payer's money, when there was clearly a smarter way to iron the problem out.

I was almost certain there was a warrant out for my arrest, so I'd decided to leave the country in as low key a manner as possible, as low key as a six foot three British Heavyweight contender possibly could. I couldn't just wonder in to Althams on Kirkgate, alarm bells would be ringing. Luckily I had a few friends of influence down south who were more than willing to play a small role in getting me out of their hair forever, no matter what the cost.

The main one being my auld pal Alex. Originally from Hunslet, Leeds but now based down in London, he had a vested interest in a travel agency near his offices in the Haymarket.

Without so much as a few quid to my name, or so he thought, I managed to blag a paid flight on the back of some fictitious royalties that were coming my way from my publisher old man Lofthouse back in Pontefract.

Anyway I'd made it, eventually, and here I was. I'd never been to Singapore before but a few of my 'more' well-travelled friends had told me it was my kind of scene, and they knew me far too well.

By sheer perseverance I'd managed to get a couple of days release to sort the situation out, convincing those crazy 'Singha Pigs' that I could raise the funds to clear the hotel bill and get myself back home through that very same pal of mine back in London.

If I'd been back home in the UK I probably could have actually pulled it off and cleared a debt like that, but all the way over here in Singapore there wasn't a cat in hells chance anyone would lend me the money. They'd be praying I never got back.

I was in no position to dish out intimidation tactics either. I'd rubbed half the population of the British Isles up the wrong way. My credit had expired with at least 99% of my friends and an even higher percentage of my enemies. A couple of which I'd bled dry just before I'd left.

CHAPTER THREE

'FECULENT WATERS'

I was bang in trouble. I'd had to avoid a Police Launch, it were either that or Changi Nick. They'd still got my passport in Singapore. Those cheeky gooks had confiscated it, little chance of making it anywhere now, even if I had the money.

If I'd been back in the UK I'd have put the feelers out with my auld pals of standing; Dennis from up on the Heath or Alex down in the big smoke, and maybe got myself a snide, but by now they too would be glad I was fuckin stranded.

I needed a plan. I knew a little about the geography of the Straits from a course I'd done back in Durham nick, that coupled with a few books I'd read, had given me a starting point to formulate my escape.

I knew it was possible to get over to mainland Malaysia from Singapore... across the Straits of Johor. No one had ever done it before, but I had, in my dreams, a thousand times, from my bunk on 'B' wing in Walton gaol.

Spanning about three quarters of a mile, the Straits were more than doable for a prime Paul Sykes. It wasn't the done thing I'm sure, but desperate times called for desperate measures. I was all out of options, and invariably I was gonna have to swim it.

The strait separates the Malaysian state of Johor on the mainland Malay Peninsula to the north, from Singapore and its islands on the south. Usually only crossed by ferry.

There was also a bridge known simply as "The Causeway", which linked Johor Bahru and the Woodlands in Singapore. Those weren't options to me, especially without a passport, they were no doubt manned up to the hilt, to allow selective entry and exit, but not set up for the likes of me. I was a new one on this shower.

I'd read in the Telegraph that this area of the Straits had become a source of contention between Malaysia and Singapore, but neither of them would want me as their problem if they knew what was good for them.

The distance, assuming you're a decent swimmer and can complete the basic swim section of a triathlon shouldn't be a problem. No one had ever swam it before, not because of the currents, or anything like that, nothing like that, It's... Sharks! Not shark infested, but none of the locals go paddling. That coupled with the frequent border patrols meant I'd have to be swift.

I was still in good shape and knew I was more of an athlete than any of these little locals. I was twice the height of most of these eastern midgets. Just because they hadn't swam it, what the fuck did that mean? None of these little nips had swam Ryehill Reservoir, that didn't mean they couldn't do it. I'd done plenty of swimming in the hospital pool as part of my physiotherapy when I'd been in there for recovery from the Neville Meade incident.

*   *   *   *

I'd followed the street signs through the town of Bugis in the direction of the Lido. The only section of beach deemed inhabitable to the locals and the only bit they wanted the tourists to see.

In reality it was a section of water as feculent as the paddling area at Hemsworth Water Park.

I marched through the market lined streets. Some of the alleyways were so dense with stock that the sunlight couldn't penetrate and to make progress without injury I had to dodge and weave and be alert at all times. The market trader's wears seeking my head like tracer bullets.

Risking life and limb, I crossed a couple of the busier roads, ones that looked like they were built for skateboards but with five times more passing traffic than the M1. These little slants better make the most of it, petrol runs out in 2019, you could see that for yourself. It must have only cost pennies per gallon round here the way they were pissing it away, they'd run out by the year 2000 at this rate… silly cunts.

The vehicles that inhabited these streets were all tied up with wire, and dropping to bits, like a cancerous old screw. My auld pal Mick (Sellers) would have loved to keep this place ticking over, he'd have made a killing over here I thought.

The heat was beginning to get the better of me. I waited across the road, away from the bustle of the trade zones to regain my composure and gather my wits.

I'd lost my way temporarily in the alleyways on a couple of occasions. They all looked alike, each street, though buzzing with activity, had no real distinguishing features from the last. Looking at the fabrics and colours on display they weren't what I'd imagined I'd find over here, all lovats and browns, miserable colours, much like the mood I was currently in.

I'd given up scrutinising the street signs, and marched forward as the crow flies in the general direction of the 'Causeway Bridge' I could already see it on the skyline. I didn't intend to cross too close to it, but it was the best indicator I had.

Jumping make-shift ditches and hurdling fences in a bee line for my destination, in my mind I was back in Fleetwood training again. What I wouldn't give for a handful of 'Dr McGill's Little Green Pills' right now to take me away from the madness.

I was the only white man to pass through these streets in the last decade, or so it felt. The bemused looks confirming it. A stranger in a far off land, they wouldn't understand a single word of my Yorkshire dialect, it would be beyond futile attempting to get any sense out of this lot.

Not in the slightest did my current predicament worry me, but the fact that I was growing steadily weaker from the mid-day sun did. I wasn't half the man I was when I'd first arrived over here. I needed to snap out of it, get back on track, I had little chance of conquering the Straits if my mind wasn't there, never mind my body.

I'd managed to settle my nerve and decided to pay no mind to my surroundings. All around me local business owners flaunted their wares. Their offspring and random species of animal, some for sale (children and animals), some roaming stray and some chained up (children and animals). Their yelps, squawks, grunts and barks adding to the volume of the streets.

The place was a-buzz with the latent noise of people trying to earn a crust, no different to Wakefield market on a Thursday dinner time.

Even the lame dogs by the side of the road were holding their breath and staring in awe of the giant Yorkshire man wondering through the markets of Bugis.

Strangers glanced contemptuously as they passed me, curious glances. What was this knuckle dragging beast marauding through their beloved town? The military wouldn't be far behind to sedate and shackle me, string me up and make a spectacle of me in the town square. Selling tickets at S$2 a pop.

Growing ever conscious of my appearance and dialect drawing unwanted attention, I kept my mouth firmly shut. The locals I could deal with, but I didn't want to see a copper again today, it would spoil everything, it would be worse than seeing a magpie. I'd had enough law makers in my life.

By the time I'd arrived at the Lido I was sweating like a YP passing through the Special Unit in Hull Nick. I'd made it the full distance through the town of Bedok and arrived at the Lido, alive, that was all I could ask for at this point.

There were numerous restaurants and food stalls lining the beach front. Some extravagant, some not, but all about as much use as a one-legged man in an arse kicking contest, to a man with fuck all money. Oh, how I craved the Townley Road chip shop one last time, a place I normally had no time for.

I was starving, but if I was gonna eat it would have to be table scraps. I'd have to compete with the local strays, grab a discarded chicken leg or dog's wing, the heat was beginning to muddle my brain. I'd have to run for the hills like the local beggar kids did, the biggest little beggar kid Singapore had ever seen.

Normally I'd have been able to switch on the intimidation tactics, or Yorkshire charm as I liked to call it, and blag something, but there was too much heat on me. A 6' 3", 18 stone Yorkshire man on the streets of Bedok stood out like a black man in the working men's clubs of Grimethorpe.

The wondrous sight of the Lido brought an air of joy once again to my person. The fresh air was wonderful, the perfume from the odd tree, the silence; there wasn't any traffic for miles it seemed, and the bounce in my step was wonderful again. The water was as green and mirror-like as the eyes of Medussa, not a ripple broke its surface.

Who was I kidding, my optimism had tainted my brain, the Straits were polluted no less than the Ossett sewage network, and it began to make me heave.

I'd lost a lot of fluids on the march across town, but I was more than ready for the task ahead, to put it in pugilistic terms I was still only 'three rounds in'.

I cupped a 'gret' handful of water and necked it down. I knew the pollution along the Straits was notable from an old Telegraph article I'd read on my bunk, that along with the smell. Years of prison snap had made me immune to shit like that, my thirst had to be quenched and I was fuelling myself ready for the swim.

I took off my pumps and tied them in an 'Ashley Stopper' knot around my neck, one used by the maritime adventurers of old, and one that wasn't coming undone under any circumstances.

Another trick I'd learnt in the nick. In fact I'd once taught it to a con who'd wanted to top himself, I didn't want the poor bastard to fuck it up and end up brain damaged so I did the decent thing and showed him how it was done. I owed Ashley Stopper a pint or two, and so did he.

I dumped my clobber on the coarse sands and stripped down to the least I could to make the swim easier, but leaving on enough that I could walk the Malayan streets at the other side with some dignity and avoid getting nicked again. My trusty gym shorts, vest and pumps, garments only essential to the task at hand, the same ones that had seen me through several heavy prison sentences.

I sat on the far bank of the Lido behind a small, scruffy beach hut constructed from driftwood and burlap watching a flock of Whimbrells dive-bomb for discarded fish and Viceroy tab ends. I gathered my thoughts and wished I could swap places with them. The view was breath-taking, as would be the swim, literally.

I had the beginning of a trickle of sweat forming at the bottom of my back, the heat was more intense than I'd first realised. My eyes blinded by a kaleidoscope of colours emanating from a million tiny spot-lights dancing from the sun's rays. Then instantly everything was knocked back into focus.

I'd sat down only to let my reserves replenish for the task ahead, not because of any deliberation with my inner demons, lord knows I had plenty of those. My old pal Mick's wife Janet had once said my brain had a thousand and one compartments with different and evil thoughts in each one, and if I was honest with myself I couldn't disagree.

My body was rested for now but my mind went into third gear. I began to think about how the fuck I'd ended up here, and how the fuck I was gonna get back to some kind of normality, you couldn't make up the shit, the twists, the turns that my life had taken.

A black sheet had descended, my thoughts had been so rapid of late I'd not been able to analyse them. I had now and what I'd been wanting was to put the clock back to when I was 17 and starting out on life's romantic road. I'd missed out on growing up in so many ways.

Life in the last few months had zipped by like a needle skidding across a record in a tumble of events and incidents too numerous to mention and now, of all times, I had finally found the time to assess things.

Everything in my life had happened too quickly, the speed and rush, the people and events; like playing chess, doing a crossword, running a marathon, juggling Indian clubs and making love all at the same time.

My brain flitted from one incident to another like the bees went from flower to flower and no matter how hard I tried I couldn't stop them. There was a reel of memories running before my eyes.

Here on this desolate section of beach I had the chance to analyse my feelings free of all pressure and outside influence. I was about to put my neck in the noose with the hope of pulling it back out again and I wanted to make sure I could face the consequences if I got caught in it.

Maybe Changi nick was the better option. It was a miserable day, a wind with the edge of a bread knife and freezing cold drizzly showers when I'd left, no wonder I'd been so eager to flee to the sun.

My mood lightened temporarily as I thought back to the madness that had taken place in the process of rounding up the cash to make my trip. You really couldn't begin to make the events of my life up.

CHAPTER FOUR

'HERON'S NECK'

I was out on license from an attack on two bouncers outside the Kon Tiki nightclub in Wakefield, but I had no intention of letting that keep me shackled. Prison didn't faze me, it never had. I loved it, a fortified land of learning opportunities. Only a fool would waste a minute in those places, and invariably most did, but not me.

Anyway within forty-eight hours of getting out I'd gotten myself involved in another little altercation with a customer at the 'The Clothiers', a pub down the bottom of Dewsbury Road, a billiard cue had been involved, it was alleged.

A warrant was already out for my arrest, and I had no doubt that any one of the residents of my home town would be willing to stand witness to my guilt, whether they were there or not. To be honest I couldn't fault them given my actions of late.

I didn't have a name or a face, so intimidation couldn't buy me my way out of this one, like it had done so many times before. Even if I had Inspector Dawson was still well and truly on my case.

I needed to get away from the mess I'd created for good and it had to be overseas. I was 'Sykesy' and everyone knew 'Paul', up and down the country for one reason or another; every police force, every prison officer, every big city crook, small time con and bent business man.

Eventually absconding always proved fruitless, but at least I could have a bit of fun trying to evade capture for a while.

Even Spain wasn't far enough these days, every other copper on the streets of Wakefield was earning enough for their week in the sun. I had to put some real distance between me and the law this time. Singapore, it was.

I'd absconded from the half-way house they were using as a bridging point before reintegrating me back into society, again.

I'd defied the rules. When would they learn? Their stupidity amazed me at times, honestly if you relied on the mentality of any copper, screw or magistrate in this country we wouldn't have discovered the Isle of Man yet.

I'd had enough of the nick; almost 13 years was a good lump of life for a feller my age. There was so much to do, so much time to make up for, so many places to see, but it all took money and I didn't have any of that.

I'd formulated a plan and as soon as I had a few quid I'd be leaving the UK for good. I remembered back to the pact me and baldy old Norm had made on G4-1. If we ever got the chance we would visit all the places we'd only ever read about and go to places we'd never been. Neither of us had been to Malaysia, if I had I'm sure I would have remembered it. So that's where I was heading once I'd rounded up the cash.

It was on that same sentence Norm had taught me all the old prison tricks that had served me so well over the years, including how to make a pot of tea without a kettle, something I hopefully wouldn't have to put into practise over there.

It had been my practice to have a week of gallivanting after release, and I started gallivanting with a vengeance. Pubs on a dinner time, pubs of a night and then nightclubs. Newcastle, Sheffield, Liverpool, anywhere I had pals from the nick. But the gallivanting had knocked a hole in my pocket and I was in need of a decent score.

Most wanted to die a millionaire, where as I should have been born a millionaire and I'd do my best to die skint. I liked spending money and couldn't see any other reason for earning it.

By a stroke of good fortune a friend informed me that my auld pal Dennis Flint, would like to see me at his place up on the Heath, he had a bit of information I might find profitable.

I'd made the visit and Dennis was as reliable as always. It was a nice little debt collection job down south. There was always somebody wanting someone bashing, for whatever reason, but it was usually money, and it'd usually involve me giving someone a belt.

I was in no doubt this collection for a scrap yard owner over in Grimethorpe by the name of Wigley would be any different. He'd been 'had over' by another unscrupulous ferrous metal dealer down in Sevenoaks who had now gone off the radar.

Dennis had helped me out and got me an address using his wealth of contacts. It turned out the debtor was notorious for it. Anyhow he'd wish he'd never ventured north of Leicester services once I'd caught up with him.

A couple of phone calls were made and I agreed to pick the creditor up along with another guy who was coming along for the trip. One who might come in useful at some point and from the same area, a man by the name of Shippey.

Pick them up? What in? I needed a motor for this one. Norm and Frankie Leach, his mate, and a feller I'd been in Hull with, had recently borrowed mine, smashed it up and abandoned it in Manchester, and then come back to tell me it wasn't worth repairing.

I made a call to my auld pal Davy Dunford in Sheffield, the smiling assassin. A jovial guy, always a welcoming grin on his face, but a very serious criminal nonetheless, one who'd worked with Ronnie Knight and the Brinks Mat boys down South and a very good pal of my African friend Delroy.

Davy had owed me a couple of favours, and was in some ways forever in my debt, after I'd lent him a few quid to get on his feet the last time I'd got out of Durham Gaol.

He let me borrow his latest runner, a relatively new Volvo, I'd only need it for a day or two I told him, he trusted me implicitly, like I had Mick and Frankie (snigger).

A mutual pal of ours by the name of Clyde Broughton dropped it off in Wakefield for me and I was obliged to run him back to Sheffield for his troubles. I'd spent a bit of time in the shovel with Clyde and as we drove back we reminisced about old times. Though younger than me he'd taught me a lot about Power Lifting whilst in the nick, he was by far one of the strongest kids Yorkshire had ever produced. I told him briefly about my plans to leave the country, we said our goodbyes, he wished me well and we parted company.

It was early Sunday morning, a beautiful, bright summer's morning and I was feeling on top of the world. A day so clear you could read the time on the Cathedral clock through the front window, I was making the most of it, as in a few days I was hoping to be out of the country for good.

I hopped in the blue Volvo 240 GLE I'd borrowed from Davy. It was a lovely motor; especially for a lad who'd never had a license in his life, anyway where I was headed I wouldn't need one. For a split second I had my fingers crossed he'd end up getting another stint so I could keep it, but quickly erased that cruel thought. Fat chance, he'd been somewhat of a career criminal and only ever got a four stretch, and to boot I wouldn't be around.

It had electric windows, leather upholstery and a 2.5 litre engine, it wasn't brand-new but it had been well cared for. A brand-new engine and gear-box, only the body-work on one side needed some work and it had flown around the country many a time without problem, Davy assured me and I had no reason to doubt it.

I turned the key in the ignition and the engine suddenly roared into life shattering the peace and tranquillity and scaring a flock of sparrows from the guttering of the nearest building. The roads were still and quiet and it was a joy to give it some poke on the way out of Wakefield.

The local bobbies would never pull me leaving Wakefield, they positively jumped for joy every time I crossed its borders.

The job was in Sevenoaks on the south-east side of London in western Kent, and not a place I had visited before. Approximately 4 hours away by car and by my reckoning about 200 miles. It would only be a three-hour drive the way I moved, flat out all the way to keep me concentrating on the job in hand. Keeping to the speed limit I was dangerous, my mind wandered from the motorway onto the domestic scene, at full throttle I didn't have time for that.

Before we could make tracks I headed over to Grimethorpe to pick up the creditor and the pal (associate) of mine who'd agreed to help me out on the collection.

The Creditor didn't really need to come and Shippey had been elected on pure effort, not intelligence. Truth be told their requirement was a 'Last Resort', it was more for a bit of company for the ride, break the monotony of the trip. Drips, cornflakes and lumps of wood like this pair would never be my first choice of road partners.

As with most debts I'd taken on I was more than capable of collecting it on my own, but I knew that wasn't always completely wise.

I'd gone to pick Shippey up first. He lived in a two up two down terraced house in Cudworth, they'd given him it (council). I'd sound him out, I thought, see if he knew the creditor Wigley and try and gauge how far I could push his seemingly good nature. By pure coincidence it turned out Shippey was Wigley's cousin, so he wasn't giving much away and no amount of pressing would break that family connection, "Fuckin in-breds" I mumbled to myself.

"It won't cost you a Carrot," I told Shippey in a half truth, "This trip's on Paul."

"What do you say?" He broke his neck to come along, just like he did at the sniff of any free drink.

To be blunt Shippey was a certified maniac, not an intimidating figure like me. He was slim, about 6' tall and exhibited a friendly outlook. A terrible disgrace of a lad with a face like a vicar's and built like a heron's neck one with a fish stuck half-way down it's throat.

He acted and postulated as if he was a big wheel in the Mafia, but he was nothing other than a certified idiot and often lazy. I'd met him through my great pal Norm 'Chic' Heald, possibly my best friend, but some of his associates, from over Barnsley way, including Shippey, weren't really for me, too lowly in their ways and aspirations, but they so often served a purpose. Shippey had knocked about with Chic on occasion and I was often in both their company.

Shippey was a horrible bastard he really was, neither of us particularly liked each other, the feeling very much mutual, but our uses gave us an element of respect.

Rumour had it he'd often fire live ammo at his employees on his rented patch in an old bus scrap yard over Barnsley way. The scrap yard was owned by another larger than life character and local business man from the area Dennis Higgs. He kept a lion he'd bought for two hundred and forty quid in the Exchange & Mart as a guard dog at the scrap yard and that was no rumour trust me. Shippey would often boast it was his, but I knew different. I'm sure Higgs would soon regret their arrangement before long.

Word had it he'd also once blown up a bus shelter on Cudworth main street with a grenade. I prayed he hadn't brought one along for this trip but would never put it past him.

From there we shot over to Wigley's yard across town to pick him up.

The creditor, Wigley was another well-known character from the Grimethorpe area. He was a much more amenable character but wasn't above using a bit of violence himself and had a volatile temper at times. He was shrewd, calculating, knew everything about everything; and he could smell a pound note in a room full of sweaty socks.

Dennis (on the Heath) had already warned me that Wigley was a double-dealing, sleazy, bent bastard and a devious grass, as was Shippey, and that I should keep that in mind until the job was done.

What did I think of him? Nothing much. He was just another predictable peck-head and about as exciting as a chimney pot. I'd chosen these two specifically for their uses, not because they were my best pals or even to be trusted.

"Where we going exactly?" Shippey asked impatiently.

"A'll tell thi afore we get theere." Mocking they're Barnsley twang. I didn't want them backing out when they realised it was the other side of the country.

I turned to Wigley in the passenger seat "Afore we get too far down the road, the agreement is £500 for the job plus expenses, Yeah?".

"Yes Paul." He replied reluctantly, just like they always did in the nick, screws, cons, governors even.

"Good, cos I've had to borrow this motor for the job and we'll need to fill the tank up before I give it back." Squeezing a bit more blood out of the ever dehydrating stone.

"It's clean, no heat on this one. I didn't want to use my own motor for a job like this." Load of bollocks I thought, I didn't even have one.

I had a nose for money jobs, I could find money in the strangest places it seemed, the turkey trial was testament to that. I never felt I had to ponce to get by. Signing on the dole was no different to begging in my book, admitting defeat. I would often pull in several hundred quid in a day, week in, week out, through bent selling or debt collecting, so why would I do anything else?

It wasn't in my nature to work for somebody else or take orders either, even if I could find a suitable job. There was no way I needed or wanted a boss, I was quite capable of bossing myself. Self-reliance was a lesson the old feller and my Mother had taught me from being a nipper and almost thirteen years in the nick had done the rest.

* * * *

ARE YOU OWED MONEY?

* * * *

Debt collection is the process of pursuing payment of debts owed by individuals or businesses. An organization that specializes in debt collection is known as a collection agency or debt collector. Most collection agencies operate as agents of creditors and collect debts for a fee or percentage of the total amount owed.

'No job turned down, reasonable rates applied.'

LAST RESORT_____
  DEBT COLLECTING AGENCY

THREATANAGRAMS A SPECIALITY

P. SYKES, PRESIDENT
Wakefield 375778

FILM & BOOK PRODUCER

* * * *

CHAPTER FIVE

'THREE LEGGED DOG'

I'd set off as I'd meant to carry on, revving and braking in a series of mad dashes and sudden stops through town.

From the A6195 we bolted down the A635 in the direction of the A1 South. I knew the country like the back of my hand, I'd been on jobs all over and even a monkey could understand the basics of the UK's motorway system if they bothered to study it.

I wasted little time, paying no mind to the speed restrictions. If I got pulled I'd give the coppers the usual 'Paul Sykes' mind bending routine and they'd know it wasn't worth their time or effort and send us on our way.

We were on the A1 South, overtaking vehicles as though they were parked at the side of the road. It was the first time Shippey had sampled my driving, although we'd been in plenty of cars together, but I'd usually been the passenger. Their faces said it all.

The Volvo was well down on its springs with three strapping lads on board. As we hit the A14 at nearly 100mph I thought we might just take off.

We stopped off about half way for something to eat at Birchanger services, a service station just off the M11.

Inside we were seated in the restaurant area around a small table festooned with little jugs and toast racks. There was barely room for another salt pot. It was all instant crap, little pats of margarine individually wrapped and plastic containers of milk. All bits and pieces of instant service, the type that was slowly ruining our country.

"Paul lad, ye need to tone that driving down, you're gonna get us nicked." Wigley pleaded, as he chewed on a slice of rubbery toast.

I didn't even grace his concerns with a response, fuck 'em I thought. I'd hoped he choked on it or at least once the debt had been collected and wages dispensed.

We sat round the table and continued bringing each other up to date with our recent fortunes and intentions. What earners were in the pipeline, who'd recently had a belt or a bust up with or from their missus. I'd hinted that sooner or later I planned to leave the UK for good, being careful not to give too much away or reveal how soon. You never knew who you could trust in this game, or any game for that matter. I'd sold pals down the road for a quid in the past just to save my own neck, and I had no doubt when backed into a corner by the likes of Dawson either of these two would do the same.

After what was a lovely breakfast I turned on the act I'd become so well practised at, snapping at the waiter "Get me the manager immediately." In a tone and volume that turned every head in the place.

I wiped the crumbs fastidiously from my lips before continuing to threaten the management with a lawsuit if they expected me to pay for that plate of gruel and that I'd had better meals in the nick. It was a fanny of course, a traveller's trick I'd picked up during my years of ducking and weaving and one that had allowed me to eat for free nearly everywhere I went. In fact some of the establishments in Wakefield were that used to it now I didn't even have to bother.

My shoulders hunched under my jacket rippling like an earth tremor, a thick vein throbbed in my neck, all for effect. I was warming up for a fight, in their eyes. I was a giant in relation to this lot, they knew I didn't have to fight;

I'd just wade in and screw them all up like paper bags. Sling the table and the waiter through the window without problem.

The bill was duly quashed, and I headed back to the motor feeling more buoyant and happy than when we'd set off. The other two almost faded away from the embarrassment of the incident, while the manager remained rooted to the spot, his expression unreadable. He wouldn't exhale again until we hit the M25.

They didn't really know it but for the next day or so they'd slung their lot in with me. It was Paul's way or no way and if Wigley wanted his money he'd simply have to put up with it.

We set off again and I continued driving exactly the way Del had the morning I'd been released from Durham nick. Zoom, sudden stop. Zoom, sudden stop. I thought any minute I would be sea-sick but I wasn't and in no time we were almost there. The M25, A25, A224 they all blurred into the background as quickly as they arrived.

As we hit the debtor's resident town of Chipstead I felt a sense of unwellness leaking in to my being. Without fail and every time I'd been in London my stomach had been upset and I'd had headaches caused by the foul heaviness of petrol fumes in the air. Here we were on the outskirts of the capital and the atmospheric change was already being acknowledged by my system. Wakefield may have its faults, but you couldn't put a price on fresh air.

I pulled up on what appeared to be Main Street. We'd only set off about eight thirty in the morning and rolled up well before dinner and in record time.

I wound down the car window and asked an elderly looking old bint, who happened to be out on her morning jaunt, for directions.

"Scuse me love do you know where I might find Bullfinch Lane?" I said with a sloppy grin, one that reeked of wind-up merchant. As though the street name itself were a play on words or indeed I already knew where it was.

She turned to face me, her lipstick cockeyed, and two daubs of rouge had been applied with a whitewash brush. Her eyebrows were different colours. She looked positively ridiculous.

She looked at me like I was from another planet, I was, Yorkshire, and said "Sorry young man, could you repeat that?" Bending her ear in an action unnecessary to make her point. Clearly this one needed her bloody ears rinsing out.

"Bullfinch Lane ye silly mare, where is it?" Her face turned a colour of purple disdain. She clearly wasn't used to such obnoxious Wakefield charm.

She replied "It's about half a mile down the road on the left." Abruptly turning her back and storming off, mumbling something or other about my rudeness.

'Sorry love.' I smiled ruefully.

Silly old cow. I hoped her legs chaffed as she sauntered down the road with the gait of a three-legged dog and all the sex appeal of a school dinner-lady. As she crossed the road I hoped she might become the Ripper's next victim, if he ever ventured this far, though clearly expanding down south wasn't part of his modus operandi.

"Tone it down a bit Paul lad." Wigley said with a begging tone.

"Nowt wrong wi' that Wiggaz. Yer can't get locked up for havin' front." I pointed out lapsing into a broad Barnsley dialect to mock his Grimethorpe affliction once again.

I was getting anxious now, I had business to take care of, I put my foot down and motored down the straight, swung a left and screeched to a dead halt outside the address we'd been given.

It was a narrow street, there wasn't anywhere to park. I'd temporarily blocked the road completely. I knew that would spur me on to deal with the matter swiftly.

CHAPTER SIX

'THREATENAGRAMS A SPECIALITY'

We'd arrived at the Debtor's door. There was no time for hesitation. The potential for naked violence was only a few strides away now.

"You stay here lads. If I'm not out in fifteen minutes come get me." I'd be out in less than that, no doubt. I'd be in no more than a few minutes I thought.

"Oh, and if the law turns up… make sure you fuck off sharpish." Drips like these needed that level of guidance.

I was doing them both a favour. Wigley was prone to making mistakes and Shippey was currently working for slave's wages at Rawson's Mill, trying to stay on the right side of the law while on license for an incident involving a black pimp from Leeds and a mis-sold set of golf clubs. I'd have been a bastard of a friend if I'd let them get out.

I got out of the car and headed up the narrow path leading to the debtor's door, my so-called 'partners in crime' remaining in the car as instructed. No doubt with their fingers and any other feasible limb crossed that the money would be handed over without problem. Maybe even a cup of tea, some bullshit explanation and the whole affair would be over. Life was rarely that simple, especially in the world of debt collection where the devil's currency was at stake.

I strode rambunctiously through the yard. All down the sides of the garden were high young cedars and elms that acted as a useful cloak to any impending crime that I might or might not commit.

I knocked on the door politely first off, trying to catch them off guard, nothing. I tried the handle but it was locked, so I gave it a bit of shoulder. It was one of those upmarket, made to measure 1930's oak slabs, a proper piece of work. I knew I'd be there all day trying to knock it through so went round the side to try and find the nearest decent sized window.

I'd just started to try and force my way through a partially opened window, but again it was proving tricky when...

BANG, BANG! What the fuck... I had to put my fingers in my ears to drown out the racket.

BANG! Another. The initial shock had worn off, I felt a real pecker-head, clearly it was only bangers.

I could see the silhouette of some old dear in the living through the filthy net curtains. It was what I assumed to be the debtor's wife setting off what were most likely bird-scarers in the house and trying to give the impression I was being fired at. It would take more than that to deter me. I'd heard the silly old cow might interfere, and invariably they always did, but this one had balls the size of dinner plates.

I carried on in my vain attempt to force the window. I could see the silhouette of what had to be the debtor join the flabby old cow in the front room.

BOOM! Smaaaaaassh! The silly old bastard had fired a very real shot through the window, it was a mile off the mark, and I'd been a clear shot, clearly he didn't have the bollocks to see it through.

I caught a glimpse of his manic expression, his eyes turning the colour of brake lights. A fat old feller of about fifty and in need of a shave and a new set of teeth. He had all but his shoes on and his clothing was positively filthy.

I caught sight of the gun in all the commotion, an old antique piece of shit, big enough to bring down an elephant, but not efficient or reliable enough to bring down auld Sykesy.

The adrenalin was pumping now, and my aggression bubbled. I brushed off the glass shards that had attached themselves to the Slazenger training top I was wearing and made no delay in putting matters right.

I ran back round to the front door, my mad was up, my temper came off a hair trigger in these situations, it was right up to eleven now. Without hesitation I smashed the front door straight off its hinges, first attempt, my shoulder grateful a second one wouldn't be required.

I bolted through the door and side stepped into the room entrance on the right like a seasoned fly-half and into the living room where they both stood with faces an inch from the floor. The old man was too frightened now to even hold up the gun, not that it would have deterred me at this point.

The old boy had a belly like a landlord's wife. It hung over his shorts like a willow tree. I'd have no trouble with a fat slob like him.

I belted him straight in the stomach, even through the protective blamonge of his gut, his breath was gone and at least three of his ribs cracked. Take that ye fat pig, I thought. This guy had gotten himself stuck in the groove of deceit and he needed it knocking out of him and now I'd got his attention.

Fair play to him, as I stood back to admire my handy work, he gritted his teeth and came forward throwing punches, though with all the speed, precision and economy of a Sheffield-steel lawnmower.

I gave him a hard left, knocking him the full length of the room, not out cold but such that he didn't have a fuckin clue where he was. The left side of his face a crimson mask, he'd play ball now.

I turned around and gave the old dear a nasty backhander. The natural reaction of any sane thinking feller in such a predicament, I thought.

With that she burst into a maniacal shriek, a lunatic witch doctor who'd just found the formula, the look on her face told me it wasn't the first time she'd had a slap, she'd probably taken one off the old man at some point, in fact I'm sure her eyes had lit up momentarily when I'd laid into him with that left hook.

She glared at me for a moment, then yelled "You 'orrible pig ugly bastard!" That may be the case but I wasn't the one taking liberties with my friends.

Her eyes blazed for an instant. She had the raving needle. Women in my opinion were the most devious, treacherous, despicable people on earth and she was reiterating my point. Women these days had gotten far too cocky; they'd been conditioned by birth pills, I thought.

CRASH! The holdall I'd brought to recover the debt crashed into the wall an inch above her head and frightened her to death for the second time in the last thirty seconds.

The old man was still so dazed he didn't quite know what was happening. He grunted from the effort of rising. I took half a step towards him just to let him know he needn't bother. He couldn't leap to his feet quicker than I could hit him anyway; he was flapping like a fish out of water.

The old cow was still on the floor, I gave her a bit more of a slap about for good measure and let her know I had no bounds.

Any independent observers watching this little drama unfold might have been under the illusion these two were to be pitied, in essence they'd robbed a good friend (snigger) of thousands of pounds, and in reality, they deserved everything they got. If there was any justice they'd finish up skint, beaten, and terribly disillusioned, lesson enough that they'd never do it again and ready for the next life.

I made my way across the room, it was done up like some old granny flat, an oil painting of a spit-fire on the back wall and a hideous green sofa, that could do with a dust.

The kitchen had the remains of yesterday's dinner on the table and the sink was piled high with dirty crockery.

She appeared to have been smoking a cigarette before the day's events had unfolded. I casually picked it up from the side and took the last drag, swivelling my head to survey the room and admiring my work.

"We haven't got any money!" The silly old cow pleaded with a newfound despair, and with which I promptly flicked the still burning tab end in her direction.

I knew different, she must have thought I'd been born in the nick. All those years in the shovel hadn't been completely wasted. Psychology was one of the subjects that had rubbed off on me like the gold from a snide bracelet. With my formative years spent boxing and in the nick I'd be a real dummy if I couldn't read people without them even having to open their mouth; I'd been doing it all my life, but anybody could have read the signs these two were giving off.

The bile rose in my gorge. She turned my stomach, not just her figure caused revulsion but her personal scent. She reminded me of the butchers in Durham nick. I could see I wasn't going to be able to reason with somebody as determined as her. She had legs like the Michelin 'X' man and a double-chin like a roll of ham. More violence would most likely be required at some point, and I was an expert in violence.

I got hold of the debtor, that's all he was to me, by the throat and demanded settlement or there'd be murders and merry hell for him and every last one of his relatives, friends and their pets until the debt was cleared.

I couldn't afford to take much longer as one of the neighbours had likely heard the commotion and was now on the blower to the old bill. Though worse than that these two cretins were starting to grate on me and that's when I could become dangerous.

Listening to their impassioned pleas anybody would think the death penalty was at stake. He rabbited on about his four kids, and being too proud to sign on the dole, a school at the other side of town, blah, blah bah! and finished by threatening to let the state raise his children if I took his money. His pleas were fruitless, it was the principle of the thing, the consequences were his problem now and his excuses made me hate him even more.

He was wasting his time I could smell the wealth in the air, he wasn't traipsing about in filthy clobber because he wasted his cash, I'd heard rumours of other rip-offs he'd carried out, lucrative ones.

Eventually, staring at me with sorrowful bags under his eyes like car tyres he reluctantly agreed to pay but needed a couple of hours to round up the cash. He'd moved it out of the house when the threats had come from up north, probably around the same time I'd been putting petrol in the Volvo, it was strange how the world turned, our paths destined to cross.

He now knew I was a man of serious intentions and there was no way they could flee the family home forever, he clearly hadn't been given it by the council, like Shippey, and his life, just like his mortgage, was simply borrowed time.

I was just about to leave when a sharp reflection caught the corner of my eye.

"The rings." I said staring at the old bags hands. They were heavily bejewelled and reeked of value.

"I'll take them as deposit, you can have em back when I collect the debt." Obviously that was bollocks.

With that I ragged them from the old fish wife's hands and put them in my jacket pocket. Her face the epitome of abject misery.

I agreed I'd be back to see him later that day at an alternative property nearby. That suited me as there was less chance of the police turning up in the meantime, given all the commotion.

He had my word I would burn the place to the floor with every man, woman and child still inside if the debt wasn't cleared that day, and I was in no doubt that I would.

It was obvious to me that all of his problems were self-induced, those car tyres under his eyes a symbol of his life of deceit. Yes I was a crook but my eyes weren't burdened with tyres like his. I'd always slept well. I'd never taken a liberty in my life, in every case I was in the right.

The old dear turned and left the room, with her shoulders slumped and her chin down. This was the final straw for her, when the debt was paid, she'd be taking no more shit, the kids would be long left home and she had no reason to hang around, or that's what I'd told myself.

I left the living room and strode calmly towards the front door. There were three ducks flying up the stairs and brass ornaments all over the house. It was musty too, the old feller obviously wouldn't let her open the windows or even the curtains in case a passing burglar (or bailiff) happened to look through the window. Without an intake of natural light their eye muscles would surely atrophy, they'd be blind before the year was out, I reckoned.

I headed back to the car, confident that later that afternoon we'd be heading home with a haul worthy of the trip.

"Sorted lads, were picking up the money in an hour or so." I stated calmly and sat back in the driver's seat of the Volvo.

CHAPTER SEVEN
'AN EXPERT AT VIOLENCE'

With a few hours to kill the three of us walked around the town and what appeared to be the new shopping precinct.

The streets were wide, the old cobbles still in the process of being removed. Old dilapidated buildings were being demolished and new ones built. It was neat, clean and very modern. There wasn't a sign of the dark satanic mills you found back home in West Yorkshire. It was marvellous by comparison.

It was mid-week; everybody had clearly done their shopping come dinner time, leaving the streets practically deserted apart from the wealthier sorts who could afford to continue dispensing of their wealth in the local boutiques.

The well to-do women of Chipstead's bottoms positively cocked and swayed as they walked down the high street, a sight enough to give a eunuch balls. Simply, simply, lovleh!

Their skin-tight jodhpurs induced hypnosis as they clambered from their expensive oversized cars.

A traffic warden stood in a trance, rooted to the spot when I shouted for him to get on with his job. He shouted something back along the lines of having to make the most of it 'brother' and he was right, apart from me being his brother, I wouldn't have a pint with a traffic warden any more than a member of the local CID.

Moments like this were rare in a feller's life. The view that played out in this narrative would have been deemed 'all rather sexist on the modern ear' by my old pal Delroy, but we revelled in it all the same, as would have he.

Some of this lot wouldn't look out of place on a Hollywood boulevard. The ones we had interacted with so far that day were clearly a couple of rag-worts among the roses and not completely representative of the general census.

Spring was more evident round here than in the flower beds of the Bull Ring and daffodils could be found all over the Cathedral lawns. Beautiful flowers so crisp they could have been made from coloured crepe paper like the ones my old mum had made and sold by the thousand down Wakefield market.

Everywhere was alive with colour and space and lovely clean white concrete, no grime and muck at all. It seemed friendlier too. It was like downtown Los Angeles with lawns and fountains and bright new concrete.

Me and my counterparts went for a quick bite to eat ten minutes down the road. The descriptive not really necessary, but to conclude I even paid, my mood had clearly improved with the days takings now well in sight.

We whiled away those couple of hours without any real problem. I killed a bit of time by winding up a few of the locals in my usual coarse manner. I'd become the village clown within a half hour of arriving, and I didn't want anyone to miss out, I was good at winding people up, just ask any screw.

I'd kept a keen eye on the time and when it arrived we jumped back in the Volvo and headed to the alternative address where I'd agreed to collect the debt. Zipping up two or three side streets and back alleys straight to the agreed location like a homing pigeon.

Again the street was crammed and all the roads in every direction had cars at the kerbs on both sides, in my neck of the woods not everyone could afford their own motor, we rarely had such problems on the Lupset Estate.

This time, and in an action that defied my natural instincts, I parked round the corner and removed myself, somewhat, from any violent acts that I might be pushed into.

I switched off the car engine and in a similar fashion to earlier told the lads to stay in the car while I nipped inside to sort business. I prayed this time the engine would still be warm upon my return.

This time I walked straight in, no barriers, not a knock, nor a lock, to slow me down.

As I entered, I winched my head to the upright position. In front of me were stood four heavies. Postulating and blocking my path to the true culprit behind them, even the old rag-wort was there to cheer them on.

Though varying in height, all four of them were as wide as they were tall. They'd probably been drafted in from the local chapter of the Hells Angels, apart from the half-caste kid, who appeared a little out of place. Local chapter or not, these lot couldn't beat me while ever I had a hole in my arse.

Even the old guy looked slightly more menacing this time hovering around in the background with his confidence up, maybe it was his entourage that created the effect, but I was having none of it.

I steamed straight it and belted the one closest to me. The biggest one, his chin had to be made of concrete, my fist reverberated and rattled as it ricocheted off his mountainous head, like hitting concrete. How was he still stood? My face the Collins dictionary definition of bewilderment.

A split second later his legs buckled, and he swayed to the ground in the fashion of a cartoon character hit over the head with an oversized illustrated hammer. He'd been there to scare me and I'd frightened him to fucking death! I exhaled a sigh of relief, now I could go to work.

I continued to plough into the remaining three, one by one. They hadn't had the sense to react and were still in awe of what I had just done to the big lad and now regretting the promise of wages from the lingering slob cowering behind them.

They cascaded like run-away beer barrels, crashing several times over around the kitchen, the team spirit now well and truly knocked out of them.

This motley bunch of fools probably didn't think there was a man alive could take on all four of them, they were wrong, this was Sykesy, Yorkshire's finest, and southerners on the whole were no match.

I had little time to waste. I steamed into the blamonge quartet again, just like I had Wilson. My boxing wit and repetition training making me too fast for the lot of them. They hadn't had time to draw what weaponry they probably intended to use, a bat, a duster or whatever, it was over before it started. The Kitchen would clearly be in need of refurbishment after this bunch of pot-bellies had crashed through its cheap laminate doors.

As I came from behind the kitchen table I was jumped on from behind. I'd tripped over the feller I'd flattened first and finished up on the floor with another big heavy lump laid on top of me. My arm was around his neck and my teeth were sunk deep into his cheek. He couldn't move and neither could I. I was mindful that with every minute that passed the chances of me getting locked up were increasing.

'If you move, you fat cunt, I'll rip your fucking face off.' I said through clenched teeth.

The message was delivered and within an instant I was back up and all over them again.

The smallest of the bunch had never recovered from the misjudged clip I'd caught him with and looked like he had fallen into the middle of an imaginary privet hedge and appeared to be learning to swim. I pulled him out and guided him through the kitchen serving hatch like a dwarf being tossed down a Blackpool bowling alley, (that's another story).

I turned and looked at the third one. The way this one had been leant on the kitchen worktop with his hands down and chin tilted had been a pure invitation to belt him and I didn't want to turn down the invitation.

Wading in like Jerry Quarry used to with a variety of hooks to the head and body and finishing off with a thumping right-hander the 'darkie' kid was dumped on his arse. It was more the shock than the power of the punch I'd given him, but he didn't regain his feet while I was there.

The old dear was hovering by the back door and screaming like a baby in a house fire, positively begging for another slap.

'I'll fucking kill you." I said stepping over the big one still out cold and advancing my way towards the slob.

"You lousy cunt, I'll fucking rip your head off." 'That told him, I thought, dead chuffed.

He grabbed, he mauled, he back-pedalled, he threw his right hand four times and pawed with his left like a big tart. He hadn't a clue. A whooshing left hook that wouldn't knock the top off a pint and a big right-hand. He winched it back to the side of his ear like a castle drawbridge. Snick, it settled in cocked and ready. He'd launch it when he saw the target. The first time I'd shown him my chin then I ducked when it set off. My knees were bent and my eyes on it. It skimmed across my skull like a howitzer shell. I saw a sheet of fire from the friction. It was a 22 inch gun of a punch. He hadn't the strength left to even winch the drawbridge, never mind fire the gun. He was that knackered, floundering, very close to sheer panic. He reminded me of a kid I'd rescued when I'd been a lifeguard on Blackpool Pier. A feller had been clinging to an upright under the south pier on a rising tide and the sea choppy.

I'd grabbed his collar as he'd been swept past. He'd stuck to me like burning rubber.

It was over. None were afflicted with resurrection after I'd clumped them, not a single one.

"Where's the fucking money?" I said and butted him (the debtor) with a measured force sufficient to get the point across but keep him compos enough to sort the matter out. He grabbed on to me in grim death.

His lips were like rolls of lino, his nose had the curve of a banana and both eyes were swollen and rapidly turning royal-blue. Maybe I'd misjudged that one a little, but it did the trick.

"Gerr up you fucking coward." I roared, still holding him by the scruff of the neck.

"Where's the fucking money?" I reiterated.

Now completely obliterated he nodded in the direction of the kitchen cupboard up to his right. I slung him to the floor and gave him a boot up the arse for good measure.

I opened the cupboard and inside were a couple of battered old Crawford's Rover biscuit tins.

I placed the tins down on the kitchen worktop, and knew instantly there was a lot more here than I'd been sent to recover. I'd seen a grand or two before, I knew the thickness and there was clearly several times what Wigley had needed to clear the debt, after my expenses obviously, (snigger).

The first box contained mostly cash, about five grand by my reckoning, and some small items of jewellery. The other one seriously heavier held about ten 20g gold ingots, serious little lumps, the type with an intrinsic value and worth way more than what I'd been sent to recover.

The old fool must have stored his illegitimate takings at this address on a regular basis, because I reckoned the contents of those tins was about nine grand in total, the debt was only TWO!. Everything had fallen into line perfectly, I'd landed the Jackpot and this time it wasn't the Balne Lane Club fruit machine.

The week after I thought I might have a mention in the financial pages of 'The Sunday Times.' Of all the ways I'd tried to make money debt collecting was the best and I took to it like a duck takes to water.

I slung the old biscuit tins in my trusty Dunlop holdall and carried it back to the car like it was fresh air. These two didn't need to know what I'd recovered, they just needed what they were owed.

On my way out, I grabbed a box of cigarettes that happened to be out on the side and told them in no uncertain terms to pack their bags and leave town or I'd be back to break all their legs, they needn't bother, I had no intention of ever coming back.

In all the commotion I'd had little chance to take in my surroundings. The place was a little witch's house I thought leaving through the kitchen door and seeing an iron pot for boiling cats and hedgehogs lying in a heap of soot at the bottom of a great chimney with an open fireplace. Tiny window-panes in bottle glass were mostly broken and the floor had risen. Doors were hanging off and plaster had fallen to expose bare stone walls. It was dark and dingy and completely filthy. The living room was chocolate brown and had a greasy square of carpet remnant in the middle. Everything, the settee, the two single beds, the table, a set of cupboards, were all greasy-brown. Manny should live here I thought, a converted chip-shop. It clearly wasn't the slobs own home.

"My rings." I heard a cry as I walked out.

"Get fucked." I hollered back as I left calmly down the garden path, lighting a Park Drive.

With that I wandered back to the car like nothing had gone off. Near on ten grand in cash, jewellery and gold ingots stuffed in biscuit tins, in my holdall, that's the way to do it. Not bad for a day's work I thought as I slung the bag of spoils into the boot of the Volvo. The lads in the car hadn't had to lift a finger, I'd sort them a night's stay and a couple of bevvies, but they weren't getting paid a penny more than had already been agreed, most likely less. I'd already decided that, I'd done too much to warrant it, their requirement had been misjudged, a drink was all they would get.

Unaffected by the ripple of excitement I'd caused, I calmly got back in the car and started it up, trying to hide my exertion. The lads knew something had gone off, they also knew from the holdall's gravity induced lack of sway that the trip had been a success.

I'd made my mind up, I didn't like the place (Sevenoaks), at all, too much dog shit from the upmarket Poodles, which was the reason why, Shippey said, everybody had their noses in the air. My old man Walter wouldn't last two minutes in this town, I thought to myself, even back home he'd come home twice a week with dog shit on his shoes, he'd be positively breaking records around here.

Now I needed all my concentration to find my way out of the town and back to the M25. No use having the score of the century to get pulled half a mile down the road near the scene of the crime, I thought. I'd learnt that lesson after me and my old pal Ron from Blackpool had alleviated a bookmaker's accountant of his takings in Hartlepool some years before, and I'd ended up getting a four stretch for my troubles.

Without letting anybody overtake us I zoomed down streets, round roundabouts, stopping with sudden jerks and starting up again with more G-force than a Big Dipper. This motor positively loved the Kent roads.

CHAPTER EIGHT

'BARSAC'

It was nearing 6 o' clock in the evening, too late to drive all the way back up to Yorkshire, more's the point I was ravenous. The day's altercations had zapped all of my reserves and I was desperately in need of fuel. I'd treat the lads to a stay at a nice country gaff, the drinks would be on me, or someone yet to be decided.

I told the lads we'd stop over at a nice little country Inn I'd seen the signs for on the way down. The White Hart Country Inn in Fulbourn on the outskirts of Cambridge.

We'd skirted past it on the way down, and even the road side signs told me it was the kind of place frequented by travelling business men, a place you only stayed when some other poor bastard was footing the bill.

"Don't worry. I'll sort the bill." The lads jumped at the chance, it was rare they'd ever slept outside of their own beds, lads like these from the back-waters of Barnsley weren't so well travelled.

We meandered along narrow country roads, crossed a rickety old 'out of service' toll bridge, and then zig-zagged again for miles through the country side and along narrow lanes until we finally arrived at an unmade private road.

I'd followed the signs for the country retreat to the letter, but I'm sure we hadn't taken the quickest or most efficient route there, though definitely the most discreet one. If by chance there had been a patrol car out looking for us, it wouldn't be round here.

For the first time I hadn't a clue where we were at all. It could have been another country because the weather was ten degrees warmer than when we'd set off from Yorkshire and there wasn't a sign the cruel winter mistress had ever lived in this part of the world.

We landed at the Inn about an hour later. It was a nicely polished gaff with fitted carpets and clean ash-trays. The kind of place frequented by travelling salesman, retired coal board directors, freemasons and anyone else with a couple of quid more than the next man.

The owner was a consumptive-looking feller who could easily have been an ex-miner who'd taken it on for health reasons.

He was a tall, bulky man, but his head was too small to be in proportion with his lumbering shoulders, assets beneficial in a rugby scrum but not much use for out-foxing a trio of travelling crooks.

I pulled out a large wad of cash and asked the landlord how much he wanted for two rooms for the night. He said it was no problem, to relax, and that we should settle up the next day before we left, that was his first and most critical mistake.

I took a master suite and left the two potential lovers to share a modest twin room, keeping expenses to a minimum for Wigley's sake (snigger).

I'd booked us in using my theatrical airs and graces and my stage name for the day, Mr Jack Kearford. He was another lunatic from the Barnsley area, and I figured these two pillocks might find it easier to remember a name they already knew. Some task for a couple of lads who appeared to have handed their brains in at birth.

Kearford had a barrel chest and was a local hard man. He was a very pleasant man, fit for his age, shaped like a barrel but had no fat on him. He'd done plenty of time in the shovel during his life, just like me. The Kearfords were a large family who interrelated with the travellers and much feared in the Barnsley area.

Jack used to go out in Wakefield on week night and then walk back to Grimethorpe. On the way home he would try house doors and commit burglaries and a couple of times had come unstuck.

On another occasion he was holed up in a pub and the police came to drag him out. Because of his reputation and well known for fighting with the police, they sent in a German Shepherd to flush him out. Jack grabbed the dog and strangled it, then threw it back out the door.

We'd booked in, checked out our rooms, and after a quick wash wandered back down to the hotel bar. I pulled out a wad of cash for show, like it came as easily as the air we breathed, and asked should we pay now or clear the bill upon exit, knowing that my aim was to achieve the latter.

My empty gesture relaxed the owner and he gave the standard reply, "Please pay when you check out, and enjoy your stay," Grinning from ear to ear and showing a row of lovely white teeth in delight to confirm it.

His eyes were dancing like gas jets on low at the thought of the midweek custom and mine were doing exactly the same, though I tried my best to contain it.

Mission accomplished, I thought there was no way I was footing the bill for all three of us if I could find a way not to.

Over in the bar I continued to keep my money on show, maintaining the air of viability for the night. It was simple really if you had the gift of the gab and I had. I didn't need a script, swindling was in my blood.

After about my second pint of beer I'd spotted a bottle of vintage South African Mountain wine on the shelf behind the bar. I knew the value of most wines and this one would be approximately R2,500 South African Rand back in Lagos, by my reckoning. I asked how much it was to buy, as I wanted it for me and my companions, not that the price was relevant. Not a great tasting wine in all honesty, but I still wanted value for the arrogant prick's money.

It was £300 which I agreed to pay and reassured the manager that is was actually reasonable given the bouquet / year.

We continued to enjoy a steak dinner, copious drinks and a few cumbersome cigars - all racking up nicely on the bill.

I could only eat enough to fill me generally. All the years of living on a starvation diet in the nick had limited what my stomach could hold to that of the average ten-year-old. To overcome the problem, I would eat a little bit about every three hours at home, but I wasn't at home (snigger). The other two clearly didn't share my affliction.

'Paul this isn't gonna end well, you know that?' Shippey pleaded. A game plan had never been discussed but he knew me too well.

'Don't worry Col,' I assured him, "And stop calling me fucking Paul, you'll ruin our cover" and then casually blew a cloud of expensive cigar smoke over his head, a smile now fixed irritably on my face.

Wigley was on the back foot, desperately trying to keep his wits about him, but Shippey didn't have the intelligence or concentration span to maintain the charade all night.

Whenever he messed up I pulled a discerning face in the direction of Wigley and made sure the owner clocked the fact that I had no respect for my pal and his blatant stupidity, regardless of the reason.

The other two retained well practised, gormless smiles. They lacked the wit to involve themselves too much in what was taking place.

I kept my money on the table throughout the night so that the owner didn't bat an eye lid or act wary of the travelling scallies who'd checked in. Every now and then I interjected a flamboyant story of either business or property, the manager swivelling his head like a submarine periscope at the mere mention of money. He was more than happy at our rate of spending. He worshipped the ground that Jack Kearford walked on.

We'd spent the entire evening in the public bar of the hotel. It was one of the most entertaining evenings of my life. Old Wigley laughed like never before; he had a laugh that could be heard on the mainland, a real old haw, haw, haw, belly laugh that made people smile just to hear him.

A stunner at the bar captivated the local fellers with her buxom good looks and occasional 'sarcy' comments. I was beginning to like her more by the hour, probably brought on by the Barsac, but I had no time to fall in love tonight. She had the glamorous heir of my Wendy, but not the finesse required to carry it off.

Shippey interjected now and then with an old story, always one I'd heard before and laughing like a demented hyena at his own anecdotes.

The owner looked on, his face was inscrutable and reminded me of a traffic warden's when caught slipping a parking ticket under a windscreen wiper, as he tallied up the bill behind the bar after each and every round. Retaining a wry grin like he was the one having me over, he'd probably only paid a hundred quid for that South African vintage and was grinning like a Cheshire cat inside at the profit he'd clear on our twenty minutes of its meagre enjoyment.

"Night all, see you in the morning to settle up." I announced to the few staff still remaining.

As a parting gesture I looked deep into the manager's yellow-flecked eyes and shook his hand. I could detect a hint of mockery, a sort of horizontal limey reflection.

He had been into us like a used-car salesman, nothing was too much trouble, he prayed we'd empty the place. He'd think differently come tomorrow morning.

I hated people like him, thinking they were a cut above a pecker-head like me. Those and a dozen other indications to his character caused me to dislike him; but by far the worst was the way he genuinely thought I was daft. He thought everybody was daft but no particular group of people were dafter than those 'up north.' His nose slipped into third gear at the mere mention of money. He thought I was daft and no matter what I said I would never alter that fact.

In my back pocket I just happened to have some excellent Nigerian bush which I'd acquired to help me forget about the pressure I was under. I didn't smoke it generally but since the Wilson incident I'd started doing lots of things I'd not done before.

Skinning up out the back on my way to my room, I asked if the lads would like some. The glutton that was Wigley spluttered, unable to form his words quick enough for shock and shook his head so hard the dewlaps swinging under his chins blew the match out. He was dead against it, it was just another risk that didn't need taking in his eyes.

Shippey a seasoned smoker said, 'I don't mind if I do.' As nice as you please.

I passed Shippey what pathetic remains were left of the joint and would bet my life he'd be left holding it and not me, it if a passing police man came by.

So after several pints, an expensive bottle of South African Mountain wine and a 3-skinner of Nigerian bush I headed back to my room destined for deep sleep.

'Reight Paul.' Wigley called over.

'See yer in t' morning.' Shippey concluded on his behalf.

In that instant the devil told me to 'Fuck em off' and drive straight home with the day's takings and drop them well and truly in the shit, but that soon passed. In my circles even I wasn't above a bullet. Another evil thought had been quelled.

I needed a clear head and all my wits about me to work in the morning, the expensive wine had helped.

As I undressed, my mind went into overdrive with a series of rapidly changing thoughts, the conclusion being I was at last making people happy instead of miserable by leaving the country, even the coppers.

BOMF! I'd collapsed on the bed in a drunken heap snoring away like a Kawasaki 500, just like my pal big Mick Sellers had been doing for donkey's years.

I'd made sure I slept with the aid of some little green pills called, Euhypnos, a mild sedative, 3+2+5, in that order to make sure I slept like a log. It was magic, I hadn't been sleeping well of late, always a lot of worry on my mind but with these things did the trick, I could close my eyes and sleep at will. Sleeping was never difficult with 'Dr McGill's Little Green Pills' and I awoke bright as a button around my usual time, or near enough, 5am.

It was 4:40am to be precise, there wasn't anything unusual in me waking so early, I'd been doing it for years, ever since I could remember.

RAT, A-TAT, TAT! I rattled Shippey and Wigley's room door, I'd made them share on the off chance I'd have to cover the bill, keeping expenses to a minimum, for Wigley's sake, I reminded myself.

It was now 5am dead. Shippey opened the door bleary eyed. Not me, I'd always made it a point to be up and ready, washed and shaved and full of life, the same tactics that scared most prison officers to death.

It had crossed my mind again five minutes before to leave these two here to pick up the tab themselves and drive straight to the airport, fuck my life, when would these dark types of thoughts stop.

"Get dressed, were off." I ordered.

"What?" He replied, still half comatose.

"I've checked us out, get ye shit were off." I continued the fanny.

"And keep the noise down, we don't want to wake any of the other guests. I'll meet you at the bottom of the stairs." The tales continued to roll off my tongue like a master story-teller.

The lads tip-toed down, I'm sure they'd wised up by now but they knew to keep quiet all the same. If any of the other guests or staff woke up they'd be made to fear for their lives, ensuring we left without obstruction.

Everything went to plan, apart from a brief encounter with a scrawny looking young night-porter on the way out. I told him in no uncertain terms to keep his mouth shut or I'd be back to petrol-bomb the place. We'd left without paying a single penny.

Moments later the Volvo was cutting it's away through the tarmac like a leer jet. At this rate we'd be home before anybody was out of bed, but it would probably be in need of another new gearbox and engine in a week or so's time. The car came home like it had gone and I didn't even have to refill the tank

"You took a right liberty there Sykesy." Shippey said, giving the impression he would be grateful if I would stop taking such liberties.

I elected not to mention the two sets of bed sheets and pillow case I had in my holdall, that might just push him over the edge.

He was right though, the police would have a real field day with a little scandal like that. As it was, they were giving me all the aggravation they could and I wasn't doing anything wrong.

CHAPTER NINE

'EUROPEAN BLUEYS'

As we approached the border of South Yorkshire just three hours later I briefly explained to the lads I was 'a wanted man' and intended to fly to an island somewhere in the Far East where there was little chance I could be brought home without a whole world of red tape. The looks on their faces suggested they thought I was talking bollocks, fortunately for them I wasn't.

We'd pulled up back in Grimethorpe early the next morning. That place was a desert of misery where a man could trample its narrow streets for hours without meeting another soul, lost and alone, and never find his way out. The whole place had an air of rejection, as if the council had forgotten about it. Given some of its inhabitants, two of them in my car, I could understand why.

I gave Shippey a tenner for his troubles, a piss take of epic proportions for what I'd led him to believe, but they'd had a belly full and a nights stay on me, what more did could they expect. He knew not to query his pay packet contents.

He had asked if he could borrow a few extra quid, only for a few days he said, until something comes up. I'd no fear he would pay me back normally, but given I'd just told him I was leaving the country I knew his intentions were crooked, I elected not to bother.

We shook hands on the pavement and wished each other luck, both knowing the chances of meeting again were negligible, after I'd indicated I was leaving the country for good.

I drove Wigley to his detached house over in Shafton, a suburb on the outskirts of Barnsley.

I quickly jumped out of the car and sliced off two grand from the spoils in the boot. I handed it over to Wigley and he gave me back £500, as wages for the job itself. I almost burst out laughing, the ridiculousness of me still getting my wages after the haul I'd just took, almost too much for me to contain. I did my upmost to appear grateful, (snigger). Along with my modest expenses.

He'd paid me with a wheezy laugh and said it was well worth it, all the threats and fiddling would stop. It was a pleasure to do business with me. He was completely oblivious to the fact that I'd recovered a whole world more. I doubt he'd hear anything more from the guy who'd owed him it in the first place, but in reality he was now the debtor, so I wasn't going to hang around.

Anyway that didn't matter to me in a couple of days I'd be long gone, living like a veritable king in Singapore.

I'd handed over the amount of the debt but kept the rest for myself including the jewellery, gold and another night's sleep, all well earned.

*   *   *   *

After I'd dropped the lads off in Barnsley I headed over to see my auld pal Dennis Flint up on the Heath one last time. His place Heath House was a veritable mansion in a well to-do area on the outskirts of Wakefield. I could only ever dream of dwelling in such a place.

I'd owed him £800 that he'd lent me to get myself back on my feet when I'd got out of the nick last time and I was a man of my word, or where Dennis was concerned anyway. I knew he wouldn't have missed it even if I hadn't, but that wasn't the point.

Dennis was a stocky, dignified feller, living the high life of Rolls Royces, expensive Cigars, fines Whiskeys, gold Jewellery and had birds lined further down the street further than Joe Bugner. You could smell the mint of dollars coming from him like aftershave. I knew the racket operated right from the top, and Dennis was at the top, as far as I was concerned. I was his latest line and doing a bomb, I could do no wrong in his eyes.

He was the one who'd put me on to the debt collecting job, and though not directly linked I felt obliged to drop him off a little drink, as well as the £800 to show my appreciation. He was lucky, normally my morals didn't stretch that far, especially when I knew I was destined to leave the country any day.

I knocked on the door and continued to barge straight in. He must have known my knock by now as I heard him holler down the corridor "Is that you Paul my auld pal. Come on in!".

His office was beautifully upholstered with thick red carpets and reeked of opulence and the finer things in life.

He weighed me up like I was a second-hand car he was thinking of buying.

"So how did the job go Paul, I say how did you get on down there?" That was one of his traits, to reiterate his questions, lord knows where it came from.

"Did you get your wages, a' say, did ye get your wages?" As well as reinforcing his questions he was always vague when he referred to criminal acts, as if the words wouldn't come into his mouth, the learned practise of a man who could never be caught.

"I did alreyt Dennis, I did alreyt." His reiteration rubbing off on me.

"Anyway, there's what I owe ye plus a drink for the tip off." I pushed a neatly bundled grand across his bespoke

Rolls Royce styled desk. He'd had it especially made, an ode to his success in the motor trade, real Silver Shadow parts, no expense spared, even the fuckin horn worked.

He beamed with bonhomie as he counted the money with an efficiency I'd never seen before and then looked at me with a new light in his crafty old eyes.

"I've got another little job for ye if ye fancy it Paul?" A statement I would have usually welcomed.

"What's that Dennis?" I replied.

"I've got some documents I need moving over from Leicester to Wakefield for storage." Giving me a disingenuous wink.

I knew exactly what these documents were, he'd got a load of European import 'blueys', pornographic magazines, the kind outlawed in the UK. It was an easy one, but it just didn't warrant the pull when I was so close to leaving the UK forever.

"I'll give it a miss if ye don't mind Dennis. I'm hoping to be out of the country in the next couple of days and wouldn't appreciate the pull." I said begrudgingly, turning down an easy quid.

"No worries Paul, but I'm sure you'd be fine and the extra holiday spends would come in handy surely?"

He was the eternal optimist was old Dennis, but I wasn't budging on this one.

"I'll give it a miss all the same, thanks Dennis. Try Cuckoo, he might fancy it." I said in an attempt to still help get the job done.

'If you play for pennies Paul that's all you'll win." He said. He was mercenary when it came to a pound note.

"Thanks anyway, but I'm done with this town." A nagging thought in the back of my mind telling me I'd be back. "Catch ye later Dennis me auld pal."

"All the best Paul, see ye in a month." He replied with a look of absolute surety in his eyes.

Cheeky bastard, I thought, but he was usually right.

From there I'd dropped by my pal Burky's place up near New Millerdam to collect my passport, the one Del had shelled out for, for me. I'd been shrewd enough to keep it well away from any of my known addresses and hangouts. Del had once made a trip specifically to instruct me I had to get myself a passport. I'd kept it at Burky's indefinitely after a previous bust when the local coppers had asked for it as I was deemed a 'flight risk'. I'd managed to convince them a numbskull like me didn't even have one and they had bought it. I knew this rainy day would come, and I needed it right now.

I made a point of passing through the town at speed, I wanted one last lap of the family patch, before leaving forever. There was surely a general alert for out for my arrest in Wakefield, but I just couldn't keep away from the place, and the local constabulary knew that.

I recalled thinking the lights of Wakefield nick looked just like the candles on a birthday cake. The skyline, a little to the east was a silhouette I'd seen so many times I could describe it with my eyes closed and that's all I would be able to do once I was gone.

Little did they know I'd made my decision and I was leaving for good, somewhere in the back of my mind though I knew I'd be back, attached by an invisible band that forever dragged me back home.

I didn't fancy being in the nick for the rest of my life and I couldn't bear the thought. Cons on the whole were the silliest bastards of them all and to think I was one of them made my blood boil. No wonder I preferred it behind my door out of the way.

I lit a Park Drive, coughed, wound the window down and spat at a new Cortina as it passed. I came to the conclusion I was stale. It was my body telling my brain to change the routine and shock it into life again. It wanted a fresh challenge and one was on the horizon.

'COMING SOON!'
Illustrated FULL COLOUR Comic Book

CHAPTER TEN

'NONE OF THE LOCALS GO PADDLIN'

Snap! The black sheet was gone as quickly as it had arrived. My thoughts reverting back to fitness and the task at hand. Changi nick wasn't an option, what a foolish thought to even consider it, I told myself.

Never mind the death sentence, the caning sessions would be worse. They were now being held twice a week to deal with the increasing volume. I recalled reading an article in the Telegraph which contained a quote from a former screw, something along the lines of 'They're flogging more and more these days. Before they were doing maybe 60 on Tuesdays and Fridays, now they're doing a hundred minimum." It sounded trivial at the time, but not now.

On a positive note my physical strength and lung capacity were in prime condition, though if I was honest with myself, I wasn't totally convinced I was fit enough to make it across the Straits, which by my reckoning was about the same level of fitness required to fight flat out for a good 8 rounds, or thereabouts.

It was shit or bust. If I didn't make it I'd pack it in, sink to the ocean floor and reside with the urchins amongst the reefs. I prayed no one would attempt to resurrect me and drag me ashore to face the music.

My wondering thoughts subsided. I needed to get a move on. It wouldn't be long before darkness came down, and the bats would be flitting and darting amongst the trees, again, in the same way they had done in the hotel grounds. More legitimate residents than me as it turned out.

By my reckoning it would take me an hour to clear the Straits at a half decent pace and with the weather conditions still on my side, it was well within my normal capabilities. I'd been circuit training in the nick, and in the run up to fights, for years and had an acute knowledge of my performance abilities at any given time. Whether in camp for a fight or not, my fuel gauge had always been accurate. I would never allow myself to be clocked like those old bangers Dennis passed off down Waldorf Way.

I'd read that the Johor Strait was once the location of two Victoria Cross deeds. Lieutenant Ian Edward Fraser and Acting Seaman James Joseph Magennis sank a Japanese cruiser during WWII. I gave them both a quick nod for their efforts before setting off. I reckoned I too deserved that cross for what I was about to undertake. It was easy to sink a ship from half a mile away with a 'gret cannon', but would those lads have been able to swim it? I doubt it. But honours like those were rarely bestowed upon rowdy old cons like me.

I took one last inhalation of the Singha air, savouring a final moment to asses my situation, before wading in with the enthusiasm of a triathlon contestant on the swimming section.

As I waded in the water got steadily deeper, wading was for jessies, I needed it deep enough to get my legs away from the floor and allow me to use my gorilla-like strength to propel me the 12,000 metres or so over to the beaches of Johor Bahru. My cumbersome physique made 'wading' a positive chore, the sand like weights shackled around my ankles, reducing me to near slow-motion.

I'd swam further in training for the second Malpass fight down at the Ryehill Reservoir, the Wakefield Express photographer who happened to be passing at the time would stand testament to that. I was more than capable.

I'd arrived at high tide, the water was calm, warm, and kind of brown looking. There were one or two boats in the waters, but they were all some distance away, including the ferry that travelled almost hourly from Johor to Batam and back. It could be very dangerous if I'd ended up in its path, I'd have to watch out for that as well as the fuckin sharks.

'No Paddling' the crudely constructed warning sign had stressed and it wasn't there to highlight the dangers of the sacred art of paddling itself, I was sure of that.

After about a hundred yards the water reached my chest and I could finally get my legs completely away from the floor, it was a positive joy to be able to make some effective progress. The loss of the floor would have scared most avid swimmers to death in unknown waters like these, but it hadn't me, it had been exactly what I was searching for.

Now in the autumn of my physical powers, I broke straight into my trademark front crawl. I knew it would zap my energy, but I wanted to make some serious progress before even considering any long term plan for making it all the way across.

I was really shifting now, I never pissed about, I knew the techniques and how to implement them, hydrodynamics, how you conditioned yourself so that you could save enough in the tank to make the distance. I didn't want to get stranded and have to cry for help. I needed to get the fuck out of there, not get rescued and slung back in the nick.

What were the locals complaining about? This was a joy, near tepid waters, not like the ones I'd swam in, in the river Wye on my trip to Wales with 'Baldy old Norm'. Those had been icy cold, exhilarating, wonderful, this was a lukewarm chore, though the reasons for my being there made it equally exhilarating for entirely different reasons.

The water was pretty dirty, filthy in fact, and full of debris that occasionally grazed my person or clawed at my retina, on the odd occasion the timing of my squint had been off.

I maintained the crawl for another good four hundred yards, I was right, my fitness was still on point and I was motoring towards the land on the horizon with a conviction I'd lacked in the past few days hauled up in that cell.

My thighs were pumped. I was breathing deeply and feeling like an Olympic swimmer until accidentally I left my legs low enough that they touched the sea bed. I felt cheated. But the shallow section didn't last long and I was off at pace once again.

With a mixture of short intense bursts of effort and a steady breast-stroke I was nearing the half way point. Any kind of training I loved, but long swims, boring long swims, weren't my preference. Swimming needed an efficient heart and lungs and the power I'd grafted hard for left me heaving and gasping in acts of maintained stamina, more often than not.

There is more rubbish written about getting fit than any other subject. I should know because I am an expert, a veritable expert and nobody could tell me anything that I hadn't already tried and analysed using myself as the guinea-pig. The most important aspect of the job is getting fit for a purpose and I hadn't seen this one coming so the job was becoming a bit of a struggle, but one still well within my capabilities.

I'd paid off my oxygen debt and was thoroughly warmed up now. My legs were heavy and my calves were tight but I expected no less.

My internal compass was as good as any you'd find down the Army Stores on Westgate in town. I knew if I veered off track the swim would take twice as long and I might never make it. I used the sun as my guide, monitoring its position in relation to the beach now on the horizon. If it veered too far west I knew I was going off course and making slow progress. If it disappeared off the edge of the earth then I was a gonner, the night time chill would see sure to it I was dead before sunrise.

There was a red buoy ducking and bobbing just a few yards in front of me. I'd been concentrating so hard on the task at hand I hadn't noticed it until it was virtually in my mouth. It appeared to mark the halfway point, where the border of Singapore and Malaysia would be if the Straits were dry land. I swam towards it, I was hesitant but couldn't work out why. I wouldn't dare pass that buoy, but I couldn't for the life of me work out why. Then it dawned on me, once I crossed it there was no going back. I'd evaded the country and the authorities of Singapore and was fair game to be shot as an alien invader in Malayan territory.

The irrational thoughts must have been induced by the sun. That combined with the toxic salts created by the pollution entering my system. I was becoming delirious with dehydration and my vision began to blur.

A moment later a large boat appeared dead in my path.

One of the crew members on deck attempted to say something to me over their tannoy, but only unintelligible crackling noises came out.

As the boat drifted closer to me, its size loomed over me in an act of intimidation. The feelings of fear were being magnified by the loneliness of the choppy waters generated by the vessel.

"Where are you from?" one of the crew members hollered." As if they were speaking through tubes, long hollow tubes which distorted their voices.

"Wakefield, where'd ye fuckin think?" I hollered back. My defiance never wavered.

It was then I realised, it was a mirage, the boat, its crew, the waves had simply been contained within my mind; any onlooker would have been genuinely puzzled by my behaviour.

Suddenly I couldn't breathe, the air wouldn't go in, there was a rough brick wall across my windpipe. I'd accidentally swallowed a load of that filthy sea water and it had polluted my system momentarily, like diesel thrown in a petrol engine. I gipped and spluttered for a second or two and regained my composure. I was engulfed under its mantle. Time had no meaning and then snap, I came to my senses. The illusions had all vanished. Without even thinking or attempting to change my train of thought I'd passed the buoy. The oxygen debt had sharpened me up.

There was no boat or conversation with its crew, my mind had been playing tricks. I gave my head a harsh tap to help bring back my faculties and very real surroundings.

I was the next countries problem now. There had surely been hoards of police on the shore behind me praying I made it past that point.

Shortly after passing it I felt like I'd hit a gradient, It was long and steep just like the hill up to the Lupset Hotel, of course that wasn't possible, slowing momentarily, my body was slowing, telling me I was now into my glycogen reserves and it was time to self preserve.

I knew there'd been the odd mention of shark attacks on those Straits, they were inhabited by a few breeds of shark including Bull Sharks, not shark infested but none of the locals went paddling.

Fucking pollution I thought with disgust, my rising panic nipped in the bud. I relaxed for a moment, giving the sphincter muscles in my trachea time to adjust. I was so attuned to clean living they'd contracted in revolt.

Treading water, lost in my body's control rooms, pulse, respiration, energy levels, the readout said, I wasn't properly warmed up. The stokers in my engine-rooms were only just coming awake but working like mad to make up for lost time. I needed to take it nice and steady for the next few hundred yards or I'd be shark bait before sunset.

Due to land reclamation projects on both sides of the causeway the habitats of some of its inhabitants had become endangered, the food source of dugongs and no doubt the fuckin sharks, which are native to the strait, disturbed. They'd welcome the chance to gnaw on a lump like old Sykesy.

None of the locals went paddling? What did that mean and what did it matter? If a trout had come and slapped one of these little nips around the face they'd have fallen over. I was different, 6' 3" and 200 weight, even a baby whale was feeling what my right had had to offer.

I'd heard those little fuckers could smell a drop of blood from a mile off, I'd seen the films, Jaws and the rest, how they condition em, the orchestra, the haunting soundtrack, De-De, De-De, Bum, Bum, Bum, Bum, Bum, Bum!

It wouldn't be my blood they'd smell, I fuckin wreaked at this point, the dehydration had meant only the vilest of vapours were now escaping from my being and crystallizing in the beating sun. They'd steer clear if they had any sense.

CHAPTER ELEVEN

'NOT SHARK INFESTED'

It was at that moment that I clocked it, the dorsal fin protruding from the water. Bum-Bum, Bum-Bum! then another. As much as I tried to block it out the orchestra took over, it was all psychological, how we were conditioned to be terrified, they were no more of a threat than the next man, belt em in the ear ole and they swim off.

Man or beast, we were all species in the same race, it never really mattered... till now! If it came anywhere near me it'd get the same greeting those two bouncers did outside the Kon Tiki Nightclub. I'd scare the fucker to death just like I had them.

The shock lightened, and I continued at the same pace. I'd assumed they were more frightened of me than I was of them and had fucked off, perhaps they knew of my reputation. In any event I wasn't hanging around on the off chance that wasn't the case and a whole herd of them turned up, there was plenty of auld Sykesy to go around.

A moment later I felt something brush past my leg. I gave out an involuntary kick, but it was gone. Its touch sent a shiver down my spine, not in fear, but that horrible feeling you get when a devious old cat brushes past you and gives you the 'fuck you' stare, or someone walks across your grave (if you believe that kind of heebie-jeebie shit.)

I hadn't seen what it was it but its skin was rough, a sand-paper like consistency, coarse enough to graze. I'd read about it, a property that made Sharks efficient swimmers. I was under no illusion as to what it had been. That knowledge made me wish my skin was as coarse as the concrete of the Lupset Estate pathways, just like theirs. I would have already have reached the main land by now if that had been the case.

I stopped dead in my tracks. The initial shock had taken my breath. I started to tread water, giving myself a momentary breather and a chance to work out was going on, when I'd spotted it again, a Bull shark. It looked about seven-foot-long, and a dead ringer in appearance for the ones you knew to avoid from the movies. Its size and voraciousness rightly qualifying it as one of the ocean's most formidable predators, it was as feared in these waters as I was down Westgate on a Thursday night.

I saw it pass me, I turned frantically and then saw another exactly two hundred and seventy degrees from where I'd seen the first one. How many were there? Then it clicked I'd read about sharks circling their prey in a figure of eight, maybe I'd got lucky, maybe it was the same one I'd been seeing in numerous locations, maybe the dehydration and midday sun had sent me completely round the fucking twist, maybe there weren't any at all just like the boat crew I'd encountered just minutes before.

I'd passed the point of no return now, I couldn't head back ashore, I had to push forward, the rock now much closer than the hard place I'd just left behind.

I'd encountered many sharks in my life, most of them coppers, screws, promoters and petty criminals. These lot were no different. I could see each one of them in these waters, all liars with the same smirks and grins, and I was ready to beat it out of them. Knock out all the shit thoughts, the vapour fumes from the pollution of the Straits. The same pollution had poisoned their brains and made them people killers. Unhampered they'd probably have never entertained thoughts of attacking a human being. After a couple of belts they'd be back on this planet and operating as nature had intended once again.

Before I knew it two of them were at me, one had nipped my arm like I had never been nipped before. The pain was immense, now I truly knew how my old pal Mick felt the night I'd bitten his ear off after a night out at Heppys. Sharks that feed on snails and crustaceans have flattened teeth for crushing, these were the real deal, teeth like needles, with a thirst for blood akin to Bram Stoker's Count Dracula.

There was no time to fuck about weighing them up, I belted one of them a bit lively right in the head with my best weapon for the job, the textbook straight left.

Without hesitation I belted the other right in the fuckin ear-ole, or where it should have been, a shot that would have been borderline illegal in the boxing ring. It must have registered with one of his pointy nosed pals who wriggled off in a display of fear, but I caught him as well in his retreat, just the same.

They say in situations like this you should poke them in the eyes, who had the time or accuracy for that. I'd encountered plenty of sharks in my time, these were no different, I knew exactly how to deal with them.

Sharks have a formidable sixth sense, the ability to detect electricity, allowing them to find hidden prey, well I wasn't hiding and giving off an electrical field enough to power the nearest local village and some.

I wasn't playing, BOMF! I threw a full blooded right cross, transferring my weight from the back foot to my fist. My toe ends brushed the sands of the Strait's floor for leverage, as I momentarily submerged to launch my assault. A third popped up, with a look of curiosity and aggression in its eyes. A mottled and a strange looking hybrid in comparison to the others with a head the size of an association football, it's clear sparkling eyes reminding me of Gardner's, I wouldn't be taking this one six rounds though. Maybe it was a Tiger Shark, but this was no time to deliberate or brush up on my marine biology. I belted the little cunt just the same and the lot of them were off with their fins tucked beneath their bellies.

The first one I'd belted was still flapping about like it had been shot, but it eventually regained its composure and was off, up on the count of nine I thought, no doubt off to grass me up to the aquatic authorities or whatever the fuck these lot did down in the reefs.

What the fuck! A Stingray leisurely glided in my direction. It reminded me of the half-caste kid from the debt collection job down in Sevenoaks, part of the crew but didn't quite fit in. I grabbed it by the pectoral fin and gave it a flurry of left jabs, the first one had stunned it but the next four positively put it to sleep. The incessant grin on its face reminiscent of the Inn Keeper who we'd ripped off on the way home. Had he really reincarnated to take his revenge? Without a second thought I spun it off by its fin and launched it about twenty yards across the Straits, with all the finesse of a lout flinging a dustbin lid down Dacre Avenue.

Without a chance to catch my breath I was surrounded again. Aggressive torpedoes were darting around me and appeared to be chanting my name over and over again like Zulus preparing for battle.

There must have been six or more, darting like fire flies in manner too hard for my brain to decode. Forget figure of eight, there were sixes, fours, nines the lot, their movements far less predictable than any of the so called professionals I'd fought.

They were weaving like Ali did in the ring, landing one on them would take an element of luck, just like it would with him. I was floundering, I'd bashed up whole rugby teams before, but these lot were relentless. Then I remembered something McGill had said 'When a man thinks he's spent he still has 60% left,' that was easy for to him to say but I had to put it into action this very minute or I'd bleed to death out here on the Straits.

Momentarily one hovered in front of me. Its little face was livid; nostrils flared, eyes blazing, lips pale. The devil in its eyes just like the old dear back in Chipstead. Sent to recover her precious jewellery, I certainly wouldn't put it past the old crow.

It had an almost lascivious smirk on its face, one just like Manny's every time he peeled off my purse money. It bolted straight for me, I'd managed to grab it by the pectoral fins, any man with a shorter reach would have lost their head at that point, literally.

I swung for it and caught it a bit lively right in the head with a faultless straight left. For weeks my timing had been spot-on but now it wasn't there, I'd barely given it cause for concern.

Fucking pull yourself together now, this minute, I told myself, on the verge of panic, and in an attempt to regain control of my system.

It returned. Glaring through narrowed eyes, with a look not dissimilar to the one the old bag had given me when Id asked for directions. This one had been cock of the walk for years in this neck of the waters, but it's time was up. Before I'd had chance to deal with it, it shot away from view, leaving me to wonder from which direction it would appear next.

It popped up again only a foot away and I laid a truly contest disqualifying head-butt on it, one that would have me vindicated in The Boxing News for months and bring back nightmares for my arch nemesis Malpass.

I threw a right and missed. The pain shot up my arm into my head and I went back into a crouch. Stepping to one side with my hands protecting all the vulnerable parts I twisted from the waist until I could see them again.

Just then absolute pandemonium broke loose. Without a second's hesitation I spun off a perfect right cross and flattened one. There had been four of them initially but now there were only two and I'd flatten them as well.

They were just flying 'abart', you've got know how the job works, I thought and spun off another perfect right cross. I'd chased and harried, thrown punches non-stop and from all angles, called them all the yellow bastards I could think of, stuck my thumb in one's eye, raked at their gills and spat at them. The waters were awash with blue murder and a splash of claret from my injuries.

It was done. I'd shown them all. Every last one had left with their tail between their legs. I'd given them all a coating, everyone last one of em, given them a coating. I was an expert at violence, and that now stretched beyond dry land. I was Poseidon; I ran the oceans from now on.

The whole incident had used up more precious energy than I could afford, so I switched to breast stroke for a spell to break the monotony, regain my composure and build up my oxygen reserves. Blood was running from my arms where the first one had caught me off guard, I knew about Sharks and that could entice more to come check me out, so it was time to put my foot down. Ideally, I'd have been getting the fuck out of there much sooner, but I literally didn't have enough left in the tank and needed a minute or so to pull myself together. I was a survivor and now I truly knew why they said 'Women and children first' on sinking boats, they weren't built to survive, but I was, because I was a survivor.

I knew when I got home the whole incident, almost monter-ptyhon-esque, would be about as believable as Manny's promise of a title fight. These were the events of a Blackpool side-show, "Come see the Dare Devil Yorkshire-man defy death and swim with the Sharks." The promotional posters would read.

CHAPTER TWELVE

'JOLLY GREEN GIANT'

I'd managed to repair and had regenerated somewhat using some of the less demanding swim strokes and was raring to go once again. That short rest, of sorts, had cured me after the intense ocean brawl, one that no one would ever believe back on home soil. So much so I now had enough in the tank to revisit the front crawl for the final furlong.

I imagined I could see Wakefield Cathedral on the land at the other side. Its 247 foot spire eclipsing the skyline or anything else this miniature race could rustle up and making their landmarks look positively tiny.

Dry land clearly in sight and moments away from Malayan soil, I couldn't wait to get myself dried off, throw on my trusty pumps and find the nearest bar and blag a few drinks before, most likely, spending the night on the beach. Maybe I'd get lucky with one of the local slants, there's go sideways you know, or so Wakefield folklore would have you believe. I'd have a clean slate on this side of the Straits, for at least a day or two at least.

I was literally yards away from exiting the waters on the beach at Danga Bay, purposely avoiding the 'official' immigration entry points only a few hundred yards away. My best bet would be to enter on the Causeway just before the barbed wire fences. I hadn't even contemplated entering at Tuas as the current there is known to be pretty strong, and there was no easy way up from the shore into the fenced area.

The worst part of the filth was right against the rocks at the Malaysian side of the Causeway where I'd have to exit. There was a layer of scum on top of the waters, and plenty of garbage to boot; pieces of wood with rusty nails embedded, old car and bike tyres, plastic bags, fishing lines with barbed hooks still attached, cans and much more floating about in it, reminding me of home (snigger). Getting out of the water would be as dangerous as the swim itself it seemed.

I was moments away from paradise. In novels what usually happens now is I go from strength to strength until in twenty years' time I become a major force on the stock market, own a string of theatres, newspapers, television stations, get knighted in the New Year's honours list and live happily ever after, but life was rarely like that, especially the way I lived.

*   *   *   *

Eventually I'd battled my way through the scum and surfaced on a short stretch of beach at Bahru. Covered from head to toe in a thick green algae from the murky waters along with a few other unidentifiable substances my brain didn't care to begin identifying. I came ashore, emerging and looking like the Jolly Green Giant. If anyone had been sat on that beach they'd have run for the hills in fear of this new breed of sea creature. Weighted down under all that crud my usually confident stance had been reduced to a hunch. I progressed steadily forward with a dragged limp that only added to the whole 'Swamp Thing' scene that was playing out.

As I exited the water and scraped the algae from my skin there was an eery silence from the imaginary stalls where my name might once have been chanted. There was no welcoming crowd this time.

Momentarily I had these thoughts, no they were more than thoughts, positively clear voices, not my own, telling me I should return to England and build a tower. Lord knows what they meant, it was clearly a metaphor for something I needed to do with my life, but those voices had to be ignored for now in exchange for the good of my freedom.

I'd barely managed to ring the water from my lug-oyles when I sensed the law. Their presence crept into the atmosphere like a gas leak. It must have been the smell, or the sound of the spinning wheels from their jeep making its way across the sands. My adventures were about to prove short lived.

I looked up and saw for myself. My heart sank to the bottom of the Straits, tangled in the reefs, suffocated and drowned. Something like this had to happen. I'd known it all along. I'd felt it in my bones, every man jack of them were in on the conspiracy, the world over.

At the very least I'd expected to see a few sights before getting pulled, another week of gallivanting as a minimum, to make the punch-up I'd had with the sharks warranted.

An old jeep rolled up as far into the sands as its tyres would allow. Two in the front and another four little nips stood up in the back. They quickly jumped down armed with their little toy guns. Those didn't faze me, guns or not I'd flatten this lot if that's what I decided, but where to next, I thought.

It was over, the bubble had burst. All my energy had run down my legs and into the sand. I was drained, the elation of making it must have masked my fatigue, only seconds before I'd been ready to take on the world.

Six of them, their faces etched deep with malice and looking with hostility in my direction. All but one feller who was studying the sky directly above his head as though he'd never seen it before and trying to whistle the theme tune to M*A*S*H, the American TV show. One he probably loved but didn't quite understand. The only one clever enough to realise that I could easily take out his army of Singha dwarves if I'd wanted and ensuring he wasn't the one to ruffle my feathers. I'd often tossed dwarves across the bars of Blackpool without issue. I'd have no qualms slinging this lot right back into the Straits and feeding them to the sharks.

"Mistah Sykes" The driver yelled in a typical piercing mandarin tone.

He grinned evilly, his direct reference to my name ensuring I knew that he knew exactly who I was and what I was wanted for.

For all the notice I was taking he might as well have been speaking to a side of beef in the Singha slaughterhouse. The day's happenings were revolving around my head like a merry-go round, my concentration was elsewhere.

What I presumed to be the Sergeant stood in front of me glaring aggressively. My size wasn't going to intimidate him, he had been pre-programmed with an heir of authority, that even he believed. He was clearly the long lost Chinese cousin of Inspector Dawson.

Then he smiled. Forty or fifty big white teeth in a grin characteristic of the rest of the people I'd met since I'd arrived and then nodded. These gooks always had too many teeth, I'd look that up at some point.

"You're coming with us" He barked.

His eyes were like grappling-hooks, rotten cruel eyes the colour of fish.

I almost collapsed from exhaustion, but he was still glaring at me with eyes like the ends of two shotguns, except ones that had been pressed in a vice.

"I'm the only man in the history of mankind that has swum across the Straits of Johor." I declared and giving him a huge grin back, one that looked like the cliffs of Dover, the same one that used to drive the screws barmy in the nick, but on rare occasions got me out of the shit.

The officer looked at me in bewilderment through his letter box squint.

"I swam it, Yeah?" My rhetorical Yorkshire trait of asking a question that wasn't a question foxing him even further, you couldn't learn it.

He watched my face like a mongoose watches a rattle snake and the instant I made a move anywhere other than in the direction of that battered old Jeep I'd be shot.

"Nobody's ever done it before." I continued to rattle.

"These pumps, see these pumps?" Pointing down to my still soaking Dunlops.

"These were hanging round my neck when a' done it, Yeah?"

My waffling was proving futile, my inane boasts wasted on these natives. He wouldn't listen because I hurt his ears. I made his dustbin man brain work.

"Oh, Fuck off!" I blurted and gave it up, immediately wanting to cut my tongue out. Thoughts had been flying through my head like a shuttle in a sewing machine and that's all I could rustle up.

He gazed at me from under lizard-like eyelids and said "Get in the vehicle Mistah Sykes."

With that he threw his cigarette to the floor and ground it to dust with a powerful twist. His short, thick bones acting like grindstones.

I could have battered the lot of the useless bastards but that's what they were after if they were anything like the coppers back home, they'd have loved to execute me there and then and leave me to rot on the beach amongst the tab ends and milk cartons

I was so livid I couldn't speak. The next few seconds swept past in a red haze that felt like minutes. At that precise moment I'd never hated anybody more in my life than that jumped up little Sergeant. I'd burn him at the stake given half the chance.

They'd done me, I knew it and they knew it. The Singha's knew I'd absconded, put their differences aside and had tipped off the Malayan authorities on the main land. Within the hour a small police boat had pulled ashore, I was cuffed to the internal hand rail and was heading back for Changi nick.

I did momentarily contemplate throwing myself overboard, but the outcome might have been more entertaining than my death, bobbing up and down and being dragged along at a great rate of knots like a scene from a 1950's Tom & Jerry episode.

Once again my thoughts came and went like flash bulbs exploding. How would the next chapter of my life pan out, so far it couldn't have been made up.

The copper hardly asked another question before I was led down the steps, hustled into the meat-wagon and taken back to the Singapore nick.

A black cloud rolled over me in a deathly silence. All hope for the future had gone.

I spent a week or so on a rice diet chained to my bed before the authorities, with assistance from the British Embassy, had somehow worked out who I was and that I was also wanted by the British authorities back on home soil.

It was in everyone's interest to get me back, the Singapore authorities didn't want me as their problem. After reaching an agreement with their British counterparts within three days I was on a flight home, a British copper sat by my side as travel companion.

I wasn't getting any complimentary drinks this time. The British Airways stewardesses were veritable horrors, prison screws of the skies. They'd clearly been made aware of my reasons for being onboard.

I looked out of the window and watched the propellers of the plane begin to rotate. There was a stunned silence for about ten seconds, then a noise like a bumble bee broke loose and grew in a second into a Jumbo Jet and we were off.

As the propellers rotation peaked and the ground beneath me slowly began to disappear I had one last glaring moment of clarity and made myself a promise...

One of these days I WOULD start the revolution and all the snides, like the cunt sat beside me, would be melted down into bars of soap!

THE END!

'Tha won't wear it out'

'I wish I 'ad a pair a booits med arten one'.

Norm 'Chic' Heald RIP

* * * *

Dennis Flint Motors

We will NOT be beaten on Quality or Service!

Waldorf Way, Wakefield WF2 8DH
Phone: 381480

- Towbars
- Vehicle Servicing
- Clutches
- Cambelts
- MOT Inspections

MOT TESTING STATION

"He had a basin crop and appeared lethargic, he moved like the Bengal tiger in Chester Zoo."

* * * *

Coming soon from Warcry Press

GAOL HAWK

'Forged in Sheffield'
ISBN: 978-1-912543-04-5
Clyde Broughton's Story with Rob Brenton

BANG! BANG! BANG! The front door sounded like it was about to come off its fuckin hinges. Still laid in my pit somewhere half way between sleep and reality, this morning's wake-up call wasn't the usual type. Luckily, I was still half dressed after a particularly heavy night down the Springwood. I leapt to my feet, the cobwebs instantly blown away, glancing over at my battered old alarm clock mid-flight. It was only six in the morning, what the fuck was going on. It was March, early spring and still pretty dark for that time of the morning.

BANG! BANG! ... This wasn't one of my pals nipping round for a cuppa on his way to the dole office or the postman with one of his now regular and apparently 'important' letters, it was more serious than that and the second round of thunder confirmed it.

CRACK! The door of number ten Noehill Road on the Manor, Sheffield was swelling at its hinges and about to burst, a couple more huffs and puffs from that little piggy and the pre-fab casing might just fall all the way down.

facebook.com/gaolhawk/

"Nothing but my crucifixion in the Bull Ring would put me well in with the Coppers"

* * * *
SCRAP METAL WANTED!
* * * *

- All ferrous and non-ferrous metal
- Best prices
- Cash or Cheque
- On site digital weighbridges
- Fast turnaround
- No household calls

Trevor Wigley & Son Ltd
Boulder Bridge Ln, Cudworth, Barnsley S71 3HJ
Phone: 723147

*** Sepa Registered ***

"Everybody knows green cars are bad luck."

* * * *

Also available from Warcry Press

Lee Duffy
'The Whole of The Moon'
by Jamie Boyle

ISBN: 978-1-912543-07-6

The definitive story of the man who held an eight-year reign of terror over the town of Boro.

Containing many first hand and previously unheard accounts from some of Duffy's closest friends and associates, this book finally confirms who the man was and what he was really all about.

No stone has been left unturned and this book does not shy away from controversy, but will aim to provide an unbiased and balanced view on the Boro Icon.

Make no mistake this is the definitive book on Lee Duffy, there will be no more 'ifs' and 'buts after its release.

From the author of the bestselling Paul Sykes books 'Unfinished Agony' and 'Further Agony' Jamie Boyle.

facebook.com/leeduffybook/

"If I have five pints of beer every day, I'm not drunk, it doesn't affect me one way or the another, but it keeps me ticking over lovely."

* * * *

GOODWOOD PARK HOTEL

WELCOME TO OUR UNIQUE 5 STAR HERITAGE HOTEL IN SINGAPORE

22 Scotts Road, Singapore 228221.
Tel: +65 6737 7411 - Fax: +65 6732 8558

- Unparalleled Hospitality
- Luxurious Accommodation
- Renowned Cuisine

Goodwood Park Hotel is Singapore's distinguished heritage hotel. Housed in a uniquely designed building dating back to 1900, our 5-star hotel is an endearing pioneer of the Singapore tourism industry. Much of her original beauty has been faithfully restored, with the Grand Tower gazetted a national monument in 1989.

Our elegant 5-star hotel in Singapore features 233 guest rooms and suites complete with contemporary amenities, complimentary wired and wireless internet access, two outdoor swimming pools, a fitness centre, beauty and spa services, five renowned restaurants, a bar, a deli and a fine range of banqueting and meeting venues to cater to every need and occasion.

"'It's not our policy to let inmates know the rules', well I know the rules!"

Also available from Warcry Press
Sweet Agony
ISBN: 1-85517-006-X

SYKES, Paul; b. 23 May 1946, only son of Walter Sykes and Betty Barlow, market and shop retailers, Wakefield, Yorkshire. Represented England and County at every amateur boxing level. Contested the British & Commonwealth Heavyweight title as a professional. Holder of Distinction and bar, Royal Life-Saving Society. Qualified football referee. Holder of the British Amateur Weightlifting Record, Deep Knee Bend 500 1/2 lb. Much travelled in the UK Prison System: 25 transfers in 20 years to three prison regions, eleven prisons and three special wings. Educ: Snapethorpe Secondary Modern, Wakefield Technical College. City & Guilds Bricklaying 1966 and 1975. BA (Physical Sciences) Open University (1982). His novel SWEET AGONY won an Arthur Koestler Literary Award in 1988.

I'm a wonderful citizen...

*How do you think I've got this house and where I'm living now if I wasn't
They've give me this Council
This is the best little city on Earth
How do I know?
I've been everywhere else.
I'm here now, right on the family patch
Yeah, I know where it is, I've been*

Nobody can tell me anything...

*I don't read Daily Mirror n't Sun; I go and have a look
I go and have a look and I've been
I've lived in the forests of North America, I've lived in the outback of the
Ivory Coast. I've lived in India and Russia
I had me breakfast in Moscow and me tea in Wood Street Nick, Yeah!
I've been abart a bit*

*I'm the only man in the history of mankind that has swum across the
Straits of Johor.
I had to avoid a Police Launch, it were either that or Changi Nick.
They've got me passport in Singapore, Yeah!
I swam it, Yeah!*

Nobody's ever done it before...

Not because of the currents, or anything like that, nothing like that

It's... Sharks!

*Not Shark infested, but none of the locals go paddling,
Yeah! A swum it
I know about Sharks, I know about Sharks, Yeah!
I'm six foot three and 16 stone (200 weight), Yeah! I'm swimming
These pumps, see these pumps these were hanging round mi neck
when a' done it, Yeah!
I've thought well
Jaws, how they condition em, a know how they condition people, Yeah!
Jaws, Bum Bum Bum Bum
They're just flying abart, you've got know how' job works.
Yeah, Sharks they'll have a look at me and think yeah, I know what to
do it, ye punch em right in't fuckin ear ole and they swim off...*